Traitors' Guns

During the last year of the Civil War, there had been several attempts to get shipments of gold through to the Confederate army, but the Union forces had men placed in strategic posts throughout the Southern forces and there were many occasions when news of these shipments was passed to the North in time for them to capture the gold. Captain Brad Calder had been in command of one of these shipments, and following its capture by the enemy, he had been charged with treason and sentenced to death, a sentence commuted due only to lack of evidence.

Branded a coward, the tag had stuck with him even after the war was finished. But somewhere was the man who had passed that information to the enemy, the man who had all but destroyed him – and now Brad Calder was riding north from Texas to find him . . . .

Traitors' Guns

Robert A. Klyne

A Black Horse Western

ROBERT HALE · LONDON

© 1965, 2002 John Glasby
First hardcover edition 2002
Originally published in paperback as
Gunrider by Tex Bradley

ISBN 0 7090 7211 2

Robert Hale Limited
Clerkenwell House
Clerkenwell Green
London EC1R 0HT

The right of John Glasby
to be identified as author of this work has been
asserted by him in accordance with the Copyright,
Design and Patents Act 1988.

Typeset by
Derek Doyle & Associates, Liverpool.
Printed and bound in Great Britain by
Antony Rowe Limited, Wiltshire

1
THE TRAITOR

An hour before sundown, the small wagon train pulled into the isolated stretch of timber on the lee of the tall hill, where first-growth pine and a thickly-tangled, matted undergrowth resisted movement and clouded vision in all directions. But there was a stream here and they could light a fire without fear of being seen from the great plains which surrounded them, harsh and empty, going out to the limitless horizons. There was still a vague brightness in the sky to the west, greenly filtering down through the canopy of overhead branches and leaves.

The two wagons moved up into their position for the night, close to the bank of the swiftly-running creek and the ten men who rode with the train stepped wearily down from their horses, stretched their legs and knocked the dust from their grey Confederate uniforms. Captain Brad Calder looked for a while through the trees, watching the colour flame in the westward sky. Out of the corner of his eye, he watched the men preparing for the night. Soon, there was a fire flaring in the middle of the clearing and the men moved nearer to it, for at night it grew cold down here along the southern edge of the Wilderness. The war

5

was far away for these men, Calder thought, lighting a cigar and letting the smoke trickle out in twin streams through his nostrils. They were more than four days' march south of the tangled woodlands of the Rapidan, where the Army of the Potomac was locked in a death struggle with detachments of their own forces, still holding them off from Richmond. But although the war was distant, their part in it was of tremendous importance. The two wagons held more than half a million dollars in gold, money urgently needed by the Confederate Army if it was to continue to fight. Other gold shipments had been sent through the lines and had never arrived at their destination. Somehow, the North always managed to learn of their departure and route, capturing them before they could arrive at their destination. Brad Calder was determined that this train at least would go through.

The fire flared up in brief flame, with a splashing of red sparks against the leaves as fresh fuel was added to it; there was the smell of cooking, of hot coffee and meat sizzling in the pans. In spite of himself. Calder's teeth gnawed at hungry lips and he tossed the still glowing cigar butt into the fire. Even though the fire was leaping high in the clearing, there was only a ghostly crimson glow reflected from the undersurfaces of the branches. A few yards away, inside the tangled brush, there would be no sign of it.

Seating himself beside the tall, lanky figure of Lieutenant Denson, he stretched out his legs towards the fire. 'That's the first part of the journey finished without incident,' he remarked. He nodded towards the west where the colours of the night sky had faded and there was only indigo and purple now, with the first stars gleaming faintly through breaks in the leaves. 'That isn't exactly the most direct route to Fort Elmer,' he went on; 'but it's the only one we can travel to keep clear of the others where those shipments we sent earlier were attacked.'

Denson nodded slowly. His voice held a faint edge of

irritation: 'How do they know when and where we're sending these gold shipments? There must be someone betray-
ing the information to the Yankees.'

Calder turned towards him. 'I don't doubt that. There
are spies in every branch of the Army. We have our own in
the Yankee ranks.'

'Then why doesn't somebody find out who they are and
save us a heap of trouble?'

'That would be the answer if there was only a way of
telling.' Calder acknowledged. There was no answering
smile on his lips. Instead, his dark eyes drifted slowly over
the wagons and the horses, hobbled on the clearing's
edge. Probing eyes. Questioning, wondering eyes. He
moved his shoulders a little as he turned his head, listened
for a moment to the undulating wail of a coyote out in the
sandy distance, then rubbed a hand over his throbbing
forehead.

'They won't find us here,' said Denson, as if in answer
to the other's look. 'The nearest detachment of Yankees
must be more'n forty miles away to the north, unless
they've managed to break through our lines and have
taken Richmond. If they've done that, then this gold will
mean nothing anyway.'

'This gold means everything, Lieutenant,' Calder
reminded him. 'Without it, we can't go on fighting much
longer. It has to get through, no matter what's happenin'
up there to the north.'

One of the men brought them food on a couple of
plates, set two mugs of steaming coffee down beside them,
then went back to join the others. Calder ate ravenously.
At length, the plate was clean, the mug was empty. When
the mug was refilled, he leaned back against his saddle,
holding the mug under his nose, sniffing the fragrance of
the coffee, drawing it deeply into his lungs.

'Good coffee,' he said eventually. 'Could be there's
something in being with a gold shipment like this after

all.' Later, when the men slid into their blankets to snatch as much sleep as possible, knowing that the next day was going to be as long as the one which had just ended, Calder and the Lieutenant made their way to the outer fringe of the wood. Heads down, following the scarcely visible trace of a narrow path, they had finally emerged in open ground, rough stony earth sloping steeply down to the open plain, out to the limitless horizons where they blended with the darkness of the night sky, now sprinkled with a myriad of sparkling stars, the whole wide stretch of the mighty firmament hanging over their heads, powdered by great constellations marching in grandeur from one horizon to another.

'We move straight on in the morning,' Calder said sharply. 'I want Corporal Elmore to act as scout again. There may be trouble. I'm hoping not, but it's wiser not to take unnecessary chances. Not when there's half a million dollars back there in those wagons.'

'So long as we stay away from the main trails we should get through,' observed Denson. 'Unless, as you say, some-body has passed on word of our route and destination to the Yankees.'

'There were only three men who knew of the route before we left Headquarters,' Calder reminded him. 'Colonel Weekes, Captain Frye and myself. The orders were in a sealed envelope, not to be opened and shown to any of you until we had been two days on the trail.'

There was silence now between the two men, each engrossed in his own thoughts. Over their heads, the wind, blowing off the great plains, had freshened, and was fingering loosely through the swaying treetops, rustling the branches, sighing among the leaves. In spite of himself, Calder found that he was straining his ears to pick out a sound on the wind, one he had lived with almost continually during the past year; the far, featureless rumbling which told of artillery. Almost, it was as if he could hear it now, just rising to the edge of hearing, then fading again in a tantalising way, lost and seemingly caught again as the wind changed.

He made a slight gesture with his right hand, knowing that it was all in his imagination, that it had become so much a part of him now, he could never really forget it; that if he were still alive twenty, thirty years in the future, he would sometimes pause in the cool of a darkening evening, and think that he could hear, far off and close to the horizon, the muffling thunder of distant artillery, and again there would come that fluttering, stirring in his chest, that faint race of blood along his veins.

With an effort, he shook off the feeling, turned his head slightly. 'We'd better get some sleep, Lieutenant,' he said with an unaccustomed sharpness. 'It's going to be a long day tomorrow.'

Crushing through the undergrowth, they made their way back to the clearing. The fire was fading slowly, but there was a pile of fresh twigs standing beside it and a man seated with his rifle between his knees, his head bent forward a little. He swung and came to his feet as he heard them moving towards him, then relaxed visibly. Shifting his weight to his other foot, he cleared his throat, making it a small, nervous sound in the dimness.

'Relax, Weller,' Calder said quietly. 'Be sure you keep the fire going. It will be cold during the night.'

'Yes, sir, Captain.'

Minutes later, Calder stretched himself out in his blankets. The ground felt cold and hard under his back, but there was a deep-seated weariness suffused through the whole of his body and he fell asleep to the sound of the flames licking and crackling along the dry branches as Weller fed more twigs to the fire, then went back to his post, his back to the flames, staring out into the illimitable blackness that lay all around that tiny circle of crimson light.

In the morning, early, with the half-light of dawn lying greyly over the clearing, they assembled beneath the sway-ing branches of the trees, now waving more wildly in the stiff wind that had sprung up some time during the early hours of the morning. They started on southward, through the trees, ten men with the chill stiffness of the night still on them, sitting straight in the saddle, or on the tongues of the wagons as they creaked and rolled their way through the timber and then out on to the downgrade towards the alkali desert which lay all around the high hills.

There was a renewed brightness about them as the sun lifted clear of the eastern horizon. Slowly, the stiffness left them, the warmth began to penetrate their bodies and they climbed one last rise, to where there was only the whiteness of the desert before them, already beginning to reflect the sunlight in a harsh glare of eye-searing bril-liance.

Captain Brad Calder, leading the men, had a momen-tary impression that there was no war going on now, anywhere, that it was all finished, lost as if in a dream, leav-ing only the reality of the alkali whiteness and the dust that was now beginning to lift in whirling eddies of sting-ing grains as the wind caught it and flung it at them. The sun retained its ominous redness as the dust cloud formed in front of it, the wheels of the heavily laden wagons began to sink into the shifting sand, and the itching, irritating grains began to work their way into the spaces between a man's clothing and his skin.

It was grim riding. Grim and hot and a nightmare of scouring sand and harsh, caustic alkali, of heads bowed into the keening wind, hats pulled down over their faces, horses moving slowly as they made their way forward with a river of sand sloughing off their hooves. Straining in the traces, the horses in harness hauled the swaying wagons into the teeth of the storm. It was a strange and frightening thing. How long it lasted, no one really knew. An hour, perhaps two. Then, almost as swiftly and as suddenly as it had begun, the storm blew itself out. The racing cloud of sand thinned. Overhead, the sky changed from an angry coppery hue to the familiar blue, the sun became orange and then yellow-white as the whirling cloud raced towards the eastern horizon, hazing details in that direction. Slowly, Calder lifted his head, blinked tear-filled eyelids and tilted back the cap on his head, rubbing a finger across his forehead where the hatband had bitten deep into the skin, abrading the flesh until it was raw and red.

'Corporal Elmore.'

The other rode over at his shout; a short, thin-faced man with an ugly red sabre scar down one cheek, a wound which, although almost healed, now drew up one side of his mouth until it twisted in a perpetual sneer.

'Get out front and scout around, Corporal. If you spot anything that could mean trouble, ride back here fast. You understand?'

'Yes, Captain.' Corporal Elmore stiffened in salute, turned his mount and galloped off ahead of the column. If all went well they would not see him until some time in the evening, Calder reflected. If there was trouble, he should be back long before then. If he did not return at all, it meant they were in real trouble.

'Hurry those wagons on,' he called harshly, waving them on with his right hand. 'This place is too open. We can be seen for miles out here.'

Time passed, slow, inexorable, full of heat and glare, and the dim, green promise of the hills on the distant skyline, seemed as far off as ever as they made camp beside a dried-up waterhole at midday. The heat head of high noon was a building pressure like the flat of a mighty hand pressing on the hot earth, full of the bitter scent of burnt sage and alkali. The men were coated with a thin film of dust, their features masked with it, eyes slitted against the fierce glare. Captain Brad Calder, calculating in his knowledge of the country through which they were passing reckoned they would reach the distant hills some time during the next morning.

Half an hour and they were on the move again, straining forward over the harsh, inhospitable land, following the tall, hard-faced man whose eyes scanned the country through which they were passing, not content to rely on his scout to give warning of trouble, alert and watchful, his gaze ranging over the smooth, flat desert, looking for the first sign of dust-smoke that would warn them of approaching trouble. But there was nothing. The distant hills shimmered in the afternoon haze. The sky overhead remained blue-white, the glaring disc of the sun throwing down light and heat.

Calder rode over to move beside the man who sat, stoop-shouldered, on the tongue of the lead wagon. The Sergeant's stripes stood out on his uniform. He rubbed the dust from his face with the back of a sleeve, lifted his head and stared towards the low hills now clearly humped on the skyline. 'We'll have to move through the Yankee lines yonder. Cap'n,' he said harshly, the words rasping from a dustlined throat.

'I know. A lot's goin' to depend on what news Corporal Elmore brings back. He's a good man, one of the best scouts we have. If there's a way through, he'll find it.'

'Hope so, Cap'n. If the Yankees are watchin' us all the way, that's where they'll hit us. They could give us hell in that brush.'

'I reckon if they'd wanted to jump the train, they'd have done it last night, back on the hill while we were in the deep timber. They could've hit us hard, by surprise, if they know where we are. I'm guessin' that they don't.'

'How'd you figure they got to know when and where these gold shipments go, Cap'n?' muttered the other. He got a length of tobacco from his pocket, bit off a wad with his square teeth and chewed on it reflectively. His grey eyes looked north and west, reaching out over the flat lands to where they lifted on the horizon. Slowly and with obvious reluctance, he turned his head away from the harsh, sun-glaring plain.

Calder smiled thinly. 'There are spies in our ranks, just as we have spies among the Yankees.'

'You got any ideas who they might be?' Sergeant Jerrard looked at Calder with eyes that seemed to be focused on infinity. The words were flat things in the stillness.

Calder did not hear them. He wasn't listening. Instead, his eyes held to the distant horizon of the north-west, where a smoke-cloud lifted towards the heavens, the sign of a rider spurring his mount in their direction. He nodded his head towards the dust.

'Corporal Elmore?' There was a question in his tone.

'Could be, Cap'n.' Jerrard nodded. There was a faint smile on his weather-beaten features. The corners of his mouth pulled in, the thick brows drew into a straight line. Shoulders were hunched forward as he held the reins loosely in his blunt fingers.

Calder braced his legs in the saddle, stiffened his back as he lifted himself a little, peering through the haze in an attempt to identify the rider. When he was able to make out the other, he relaxed a little. Even from that distance it was possible to see the grey uniform, plastered with dust but still recognizable.

Elmore reined his mount savagely as he reached the front of the train. Only his eyes looked out from the mask of sweat and dust which covered his face. He was breathing heavily, swaying weakly in the saddle, but his right arm still came up swiftly in a salute.

'What is it, man?' Calder asked sharply. 'What did you find?'

The other pointed. 'Those hills yonder are crawlin'

with Yankees. Must be a couple of companies of 'em, watching the trails goin' through.'

Calder thinned his lips. Quiet, steady, he lifted his fierce gaze from the man in front of him, to the hills that lay bathed in the lowering sunglow. Damn and double damn those blasted Northerners, he thought savagely. He had never expected so large a force to be as far south as this, well beyond their lines on this sector. There could, in his mind, be only one explanation for this. Somehow, they must have heard of the gold shipment going through and they were swiftly closing all of the routes, to prevent it from reaching its destination. There was a faint tremor of excitement in his hands as they rested on the saddlehorn, close to the butt of the rifle.

'You saw them?' he asked eventually, switching his glance to Elmore.

The Corporal shook his head slowly. 'Saw their sign, Cap'n. Heard some of 'em in the brush. Tried to scout around 'em, to see if there is a trail through their lines. I reckon the only way is to move south and then turn back north, once we've cleared the hills.'

Calder turned that over in his mind, pondering for a long moment, before finally rejecting the idea. 'Too far,' he murmured. 'It would add more'n two days to our journey. We can't afford to lose that much time. Men are depending on us getting this gold through.'

A moment of decision. The wrong one at this time and it could mean the end for all of them and another lot of gold in the coffers of the Northern Army.

'You going to ride on through those hills, Captain?' asked Lieutenant Denson.

'We've got to.' There was no going back on it now. The decision, for good or ill, had been taken. He straightened up in the saddle, squaring his shoulders. 'Could be that they're expecting us to move through the desert to the south and they'll be watching that route. Nobody in his right mind is going to try to drive a couple of heavily laden wagons through their lines.'

There was no argument. Each man realized that their lives were in the balance, that the order had been given. With the sun gleaming redly in their eyes, they rode towards the distant hills. By nightfall, they were still more than ten miles from them, still in the desert, in an area of yellow grass spiked here and there with silversword. It was rough, inhospitable land, and being so close to the hills they could not afford to light a fire, were forced to eat and sleep cold.

Silence hung over the camp like a sable shroud. Captain Calder sat with his back against one of the wooden wheels of a wagon, relaxing a little, his shoulders hunched forward as he stared off into the dwindling blue-crimson glow of the swiftly-dying sunset. His head was now upright, eyes alert. He did not turn his head when Sergeant Jerrard came forward, footsteps muffled in the shifting sand.

'They must be moving, sir. Probably heading out into the hills, hoping to move around the rear of our lines and then cut north.'

Calder stirred a little. 'You think that's why they're there, Sergeant?'

'I'm almost sure of it, Cap'n. Could be, though, that it might have been safer to go the roundabout route, even if it meant losing a couple of days on the way. I mean – what's losing two days beside losing the gold and maybe our lives in the process?'

'I've already made my decision, Sergeant.' Again, there was that sharp edge of irritation. 'Use your head a little, Sergeant. Elmore can scout ahead tomorrow, and bring us back news of whether they are there or whether they've pulled out, moving south perhaps, then swinging east to hit our men from the rear.'

'I've got a feeling, Sir. One I don't like. I had it once

before, when we were hit by the Yankees, hit hard. I saw men drop on both sides of me. They had us caught in that goddamned Wilderness, with nowhere to run, so that we could only stand our ground and get shot to pieces.'

'Everybody feels like that at some time or another,' Calder said tightly. 'It means nothing. Get some rest.'

'But – but, Captain —'

'Yes?'

'Well . . . You can never be sure what these damned Yankees know, can you, sir?'

'No.' Captain Calder rubbed a hand over his forehead. He shrugged. 'You can't, Sergeant.' He pulled up the high collar of his coat. 'So there's no sense in worrying about it right now. There are two men on watch and they'll be relieved at three-hour intervals throughout the night. So long as they stay awake, we should be safe from a surprise attack. In the morning we'll work our way through those hills.'

For a long period, Sergeant Jerrard sat quite still, his profile with the strong, aquiline nose, just visible in the darkness. He cleared his throat with a nervous, hesitant sound, made as if to speak again, and then got to his feet and slipped swiftly away into the shrouding darkness.

How long Captain Brad Calder sat alone, with only the two sentries stirring around him in the limitless blackness and the faint movement of the wind as it sighed through the silversword, he did not know. His limbs were chilled and numbed by the cold night air and after a while, he seemed to hear other sounds, distant and far-removed, right at the very limit of his hearing. Once, too, he thought he saw a flicker of firelight, far off on a low ridge, but a moment later it was gone, a brief spark, and he could not be sure of what he had seen or imagined.

At last, he got clumsily to his feet, moved around to the front of the wagon, slid between his blankets, staring up at the foaming, yeasty ferment of the starry heavens over his head, turning his thoughts in on themselves, wondering if he had made the right decision, if indeed, there was a right decision for him to make in the circumstances.

Morning, early, and in the faint grey light streaking the cast, they ate their rations, hitched up the horses to the wagons and moved out once more. There were no trees here, only scrub and tuftgrass and patches of saltweed among the spiking silversword. Further on were the hills, slumbering in the first light of the new day. Calder stared ahead, searching the area from side to side. Corporal Elmore had ridden out before dawn, was somewhere in the hills by now. In the distance, over the hills, hung a bank of dark, turgescent cloud. When that storm broke, he reflected, it would be all in the hills with very little on the plain.

Clear and cool, the light of the new day increased and with it, the feeling of apprehension and insecurity. From the hills they would be clearly visible if the Yankees had sentries out, watching this stretch of ground. Minutes passed. The creak of wood and leather as the wagons rolled forward was the only sound to break the clinging stillness. The men rode in silence, easing their stiff limbs in the saddle. There was a renewed burst of brightness over everything as the sun rose at their backs, leaping up into the heavens in a single bound. Warmth began to penetrate their bodies, easing the cramp and the stiffness. Ahead of them, the ground dropped in a smooth sweep beyond a steep rise and beyond there lay only the green, shadow-clogged land which divided the plain from the hills. The faint, dim trail, grey-white, snaked through it and then up into the hills where it seemed to broaden into a wider track.

Leading the company, Captain Brad Calder had the momentary impression that the timber which lay on the hills was empty of life. Not a sound disturbed the quiet which lay over everything. Not even a bird sounded inside those tall trees. Too quiet. There was no feeling of the enemy close as they made their way up into the timber. Thirty feet in and the thick, tangled woodland had closed about them, shutting off all sight about them. Thickets and heavy brush lay on either side of the trail. The horses strained against the traces, dragging the heavy wagons up over the rough, uneven ground. The red-bodied pines lifted clear to the sky, their uppermost branches success-fully cutting off the sunlight, so that only a pale green glow managed to filter down to the ground, touching their faces with a nauseous colour. Beneath their feet, as Calder and Denson rode through the rough tangle on either side of the road, their eyes alert, the needles of pine made a thick, dense cushion which muffled the hoofbeats of their horses, making scarcely a sound, and except for the faint metal jingle of their harnesses and the occasional chukkering of their horse's lips and the now-and-then sharp clash of a woodpecker's bill somewhere off among the trees, a deep, deathly silence lay over everything, among the aromatic timbered reaches of the forest.

Slowly, they forced their way forward. Here and there long, slender tendrils of the tall, thin saplings, whipped back and struck them savagely across arms and face and shoulders.

They were well into the trees, moving up to the summit when they first heard the sounds of an oncoming rider. Holding up his right hand he stopped the column. Dust swirled briefly in the roadway ahead. The rider seemed to be coming on swiftly, not slowing, although he must have noticed the column directly in front of him. Tightness gripped Calder. He strained his vision to peer through the green dimness and the dust, to make out the identity of the oncoming rider before he gave the order to take up battle positions.

Then, abruptly, the horse slid to a halt, the rider slumped forward in the saddle, the reins hanging loosely, almost touching the ground. Dismounting, Brad Calder went forward, caught the man as he slipped sideways, falling from the saddle, hitting the ground hard in spite of Calder's steadying hand.

Lieut. Denson came forward, bent, then straightened. 'Dead, Captain?'

'No, but he's goin' fast.' Calder stared into the Corporal's face. There was blood on his jacket, soaking through the dust and the cloth. Carefully, he opened the tunic, pulled aside the blood-stained shirt, noticed the two bullet holes just below the ribs, felt a sense of shock. Abruptly, it passed and a feeling of strange foreboding, of inevitability, went through him. There was no sound from the brush around them, no rustle in the tangled under-growth, yet he knew, as surely as if he could see them, that the enemy were there, waiting, all around them.

Corporal Elmore uttered a low, soft sigh. For a moment his body ached rigidly, then relaxed. The lines of strain which had twisted his face under the mask of sweat and dust, were suddenly smoothed away. Gently, Calder closed the open, staring eyes, got a trifle unsteadily to his feet. Quickly, he snapped his orders, the men took up their positions on either side of the wagons and they moved forward again, rifles loaded, ready.

They were under fire before they had gone fifty yards and Calder saw Travis, seated on the leading wagon go down, the reins dropping from nerveless fingers, his body slumping sideways as the horses reared. Then, miracu-lously, he had forced himself back upright, was reaching out for the reins again before they could slip free of the wagon, was hauling back on them, his face grimacing with agony, eyes wide and staring in the green gloom.

Instinctively he dropped from the saddle, hit the ground and rolled over, shoulders crashing into the thick undergrowth. The smell of gunpowder lay thickly in the air now. The rest of the men were out of their saddles, lying in the tough grass, firing at blue-coated shadows which showed themselves in fleeting glimpses through the undergrowth and the swirling dust and smoke. The din of gunfire lifted to a crackling, spiteful crescendo, seemed to be coming from all about them. A bullet struck the tongue of the wagon, threw off a splinter of wood and ricocheted into the brush, striking the earth within inches of his head as he pulled himself down.

There were too many of the enemy for them to have a chance in hell of breaking through. The thought pounded incessantly through his mind. The knowledge that he had deliberately led the column into a trap, that all was lost, even if some of them managed to escape with their lives, was a searing agony in his mind.

Across the trail, Lieutenant Denson was firing slowly and methodically at the enemy whenever they showed themselves. A wild cry in the brush told of death striking one of the Yankees, of a bullet ripping through cloth, then flesh and muscle and bone.

He had a small moment of panic as he lay there, listening to the rustle of the bullets through air and grass and the creepy feeling made him jerk his legs away from the trail, to wriggle further into the undergrowth, keeping well down, using his forearms to drag himself forward. The Yankees, he thought savagely, had known he and the wagon train would be passing this point. There was no other reason for them to be there in such large numbers. He knew this now with a sick certainty, knew that his mission had been betrayed to the enemy by someone back at Headquarters.

The firing swung round. The main weight of it seemed to be smashing against the wagons from the other side of the trail, although there were some shots coming from behind, indicating that the enemy had worked their way around them, had now cut off their line of retreat. He crouched low in the brush, sucking in great breaths to relieve the dry, rasping torment in his throat and lungs and he wondered as he crouched there whether their own fire had thinned the enemy's ranks at all.

Sergeant Jerrard and three of the men were crouched beneath the first wagon, firing steadily into the bushes, aiming for the spurting muzzle flashes which gave away the positions of the enemy infantrymen. Two men firing while the other two reloaded. They could manage a dozen shots every sixty seconds and if all of them counted, they must be inflicting grievous casualties on the enemy.

The firing from the wagon slackened. Out of the corner of his eye, he saw that two of the men had fallen, unmoving, their bodies slumped against the inner sides of the wheels. Jerrard was still there, face blackened by the smoke while shots came from the rear wagon. But the opposing fire rose savagely, came forward and slackened, then lifted in violence once more. The Yankees were moving in, knew they had them pinned down, that there was no direction in which they could move. The smoke thickened, whirled around them, partially obliterating the trail and he realized, with a faint shock, that there was no answering fire from the spot where Lieutenant Denson had gone down. He strained his vision to peer through the greyness, then saw the other's head and shoulders, leaning out of the tangled brush towards the trail, knew by the stillness that Denson was dead and something clicked into place in his mind, sharp and painful in its searing reality. Six men left now. There was no sign of Travis. He might have been dead too, for all he knew.

Lying full length behind a rotted stump, his rifle gripped tightly in his hands. he stared off into the tangled greenness, heard the harsh shouting of orders from among the trees. Out of the blankness at the end of the trail, blurred and indistinct in the smoke, several blue-clad figures emerged and began to move swiftly towards them.

Calder felt as though an icy hand had suddenly reached

in and clutched his heart in a numbing grip, squeezing it tightly, shutting off the blood from his veins. For an instant he saw himself as something alien, which had no right to be there, knew that he had been staring death in the face for many minutes now, seeing his men die one by one in this futile attempt to defend the gold wagons and he flinched inwardly every time death, invisible and swift, moved with a faint hum through the air close to his head. His lips curled into a snarl of ironic anger, anger at the authority which had ordered them on this mission without taking care that news of it had not been given to the enemy. Somebody back at Headquarters had known they were riding to their deaths the moment they had left their lines and headed into the desert. And at the moment, the death moving in swiftly on them, he wanted only one thing: to get away from there, to move into the under-growth and escape, so that he might get back to Headquarters and find out for himself who this traitor was, so that he might see justice done, so that in some small way, he might avenge these men who had ridden out with him and who were now dying because of the act of one man.

He slithered forward, ears deafened by the madness of rifle fire. Bullets sang and hummed over his head with a faint, ineffable sound, like a swarm of insects. Someone, close by, gave up a loud cry and he knew that another of his men had died. From back in the line of trees which grew right up to the edge of the track, the Yankee fire swept over the small group of men still firing among the wagons. It was impossible for anyone to live under that concentrated volley, searching, deadly, pecking at the wagons, kicking up tiny spurts of dust along the trail. He saw Jerrard, the three stripes just visible on his arm, lift himself stubbornly from under the lead wagon, move out into the open, still defiant, still loading and firing, ignor-ing the bullets that whined about him. Out on the fleeting

edge of vision he saw Jerrard run forward, stumbling along
the track, driving on as though all of the devils in hell were
on his tail. He was hit twice, continued to stagger forward,
yelling savagely, insanely, as he moved. Then he was hit for
a third time, high up in the chest. Calder saw him stop as
though he had run into an invisible wall, saw him reach up
and clutch at his torn chest, the blood beginning to trickle
between his stiffened fingers. Slowly, he tottered forward,
legs losing their power, unable to bear his weight. His
finger, on the trigger of the rifle, somehow succeeded in
pushing down with the last ounce of strength in his body.
A blue-coated figure yelled loudly, fell in front of Jerrard
as the Sergeant went down, dropping on to his face, his
outstretched fingers clutched at the earth in the last
convulsion of death. The thought flitted across Calder's
mind that he ought to do likewise, fire on the enemy and
hope to take some of them with him before he, too, died.
But he knew it would be useless, that he would give his life
for nothing. The only thought in his mind now was to stay
alive, somehow, so that he might hunt down the man who
had betrayed them, see that justice was done, and that
these men had not died in vain. He lay low, hugging the
ground, not moving, listening to the sounds of men crashing through the undergrowth, the crackle of brush snap-
ping under their feet, their yells as they converged on the
trail.

Very slowly he edged into the deeper underbrush. Off
to his left he heard the voice of the Yankees as they
swarmed around the wagons. Every muscle in him was so
tight that it spread a vast ache through his body and the
large muscles of his thighs were twisted and knotted in
cramp. His mind seemed very clear and sharp and it was
as if it magnified every tiny sound, making them of an
unnatural loudness and importance. He followed the
movements of the men with his mind, searching with eyes
and ears, knowing that if they once suspected there was

anyone alive, they would hunt him down and kill him, or
take him prisoner and at that moment he was not certain
which of these alternatives would be the worse. Hesitating
for only a moment, he crawled on. His hand came down
hard on a ragged branch of thorn and his weight drove
one of the long, sharp-barbed thorns deep into the flesh
of his palm. He leaned over on his other arm, gritting his
teeth tightly together, seized the branch where it was still
sticking to his hand and withdrew the thorn with a slow
motion. A gush of warm blood spilled over his hand,
oozing swiftly from the wound. Sucking it for a moment,
he pulled out his neckpiece and wrapped it tightly around
his hand, closing his fist on it. Very slowly, he moved on
into the trees, away from the trail. There was no way of
saving that gold now. One more shipment had fallen into
the enemy's hands and the Army which had needed it so
desperately, would have to fight on without it. Maybe,
some time in the future, another train would try to work
their way through the Northern lines and it might
succeed. Now he wanted one thing; to escape. The weight
against him was too great and his chances too slim. Back
in his head was the knowledge that perhaps the enemy
might be watching every part of these hills, but he
dismissed the idea. If he could get a horse – he put the
almost impossible idea away from him, waited until he had
crawled fifty yards or so away from the track, and then
pushed himself to his feet, began to move more quickly
now, making as little noise as possible.

Blundering through the trees, he reached the small
clearing near the edge of the timber almost before he was
aware of it. The snicker of a horse pulled him up in time
and he crouched down behind the tangle of thorn. There
were five horses there, he noticed, tethered to a rope
strung between a couple of trees. He cast about him, looking for the man who would undoubtedly be watching
them, saw no one. He stood there for several minutes, like

a man exhausted beyond the ability to move a muscle, his breath rasping in his throat, his palm paining him where the thorn had driven in deep. Then, a moment later, he saw the man's shape move on the edge of the clearing. The other had his back to him, was staring out across the wastelands just visible beyond the fringe of pine. The smell of cigar smoke reached across the clearing to him and in spite of the pain in his body and the tight web of tension in his mind, he half smiled to himself. Smoking on duty. His luck seemed to have held. The one man in the regiment, the bad penny who could not be really trusted whenever there were no officers around, was in charge of these horses. Carefully, he pulled the pistol from his belt, reversed it in his hand. There had to be no noise. He could not afford to alarm any of the others who might be close by. Moving through the brush on soft feet, he came up behind the man. Some hidden instinct half-warned the other and he was on the point of swinging round, turning his head, when the butt of the pistol crashed down with a sickening force on the back of his head. Calder caught him as he fell, eased the inert body to the ground. One of the horses whinnied harshly, kicked skittishly, jerking on the rope.

Choosing one with a water bottle hanging from the saddlehorn, he swung himself up into the saddle, jerked the rope free, kicked at the horse's flanks, sending it through the thin fringe of trees, down the slope beyond, out over the hard ground, through the clumps of brush and silversword. A trail of dust lifted behind him and a solitary shot followed him as he rode into the glaring sunlight.

'Captain Calder?' The voice was hard, official.

Calder squared himself, looked across at the tall, thin-faced man in the Major's uniform, felt a curious stiffening in his mind as he nodded. 'Yes, sir.'

'You will accompany me, Captain. I understand that you have waived your claim to a general court-martial, that you will accept regimental proceedings.'

'Yes.'

'Good. I want you to understand that I am here to help you with your defence. I am Major Thoroton. The charge which has been brought against you is treason. You understand that?'

'Treason?' He sucked in a sharp breath, lips suddenly pulled tightly together. 'But I deny that absolutely. There is no truth in that whatsoever.'

'Do you deny that you were the only survivor of the wagon train carrying half a million dollars' worth of gold through the Northern lines?'

'No, but I fail to see where that brands me as a traitor. I've already tried to explain that to the Colonel. Somebody had to get back and give word of what happened, warn the company that there is a traitor among us who has been passing information to the Yankees. I could do nothing to save the men or the gold. The enemy were waiting for us, were too strong for us.'

The Major's tone was still cool, impersonal. 'Then you claim that it was not you who imparted the information concerning details of the route of the shipment to the enemy?'

'Certainly.' There was a vehement tone now overlaying the other's voice. 'I did everything I possibly could in the circumstances. Do you honestly think that if I were the one who betrayed this secret to the enemy, I would have ridden back here? Surely, I would have stayed with the enemy when I had the chance.'

'That,' said Major Thoroton, 'may be a point in your defence. If you wish me to make it.'

'Of course I want you to make it.' Calder's voice was hard, raised a little in pitch and volume. 'I came back to warn everyone that there is a traitor in the ranks. And what happens? I find that I've been charged with treason myself. I came back to find that man, and kill him. Nine men, good men, died out there because of him. I've got good reasons for being here now. When I find that man, I mean to carry out the sentence on him.'

Thoroton sighed. He touched the other on the arm. 'Let's go,' he said softly.

Calder did as he was told, silently and mechanically, withdrawn, thinking his own thoughts. He scarcely seemed aware of the fact that the court had convened, until Major Thoroton cleared his throat, to offer the defence. Then he stirred himself, grew aware that Colonel Weekes was addressing him.

'You say, Captain Calder, that the plan to take the gold shipment south of our positions, across the Flats and then through the hills, was known to the enemy, possibly before you rode out of here?'

'No, sir.' Calder pressed his lips tightly together, stared at the other. 'They *knew*.'

'Captain Calder.' The Colonel leaned back in his chair, eyed him closely. There was a strange look on his face. 'Only three men knew the contents of those sealed orders before you moved out. Captain Frye, myself and you. I have absolute trust in Captain Frye. He has been my personal aide for more than six years. I know that I am not the spy you claim to be present in our ranks. That leaves only one person, yourself. The very fact that you were the only survivor of that column, that you escaped unharmed, merely serves to strengthen my view that you are guilty of this charge which has, quite rightly, been brought against you. The penalty for treason is, of course, death. This is the verdict of this court. It will be transmitted to Field Headquarters for approval, and the sentence will then be carried out. This is a problem which had faced us for far too long, this flagrant betrayal of our secrets to the enemy. More than two million dollars in gold has fallen into the

Northerners' hands over the past seven months, money which was urgently needed so that we might prolong the fighting. Speaking for myself, I trust that the verdict will be speedily approved, that it may be carried out here as an example.'

During the two weeks that followed, two weeks in which the news worked its way through the various channels from Field Headquarters, Brad Calder tried to force himself to understand what was happening, but events scarcely seemed to touch him, imprinting themselves only on the very edge of his mind, on the outer rim of awareness.

Then there came a day when he was summoned back in front of Colonel Weekes. The other sat hunched forward in his chair, his grey hair gleaming in the yellow flickering glow of the lantern on the table. The two sentries went outside the tent and the two men were alone.

'Calder.' The Colonel's voice was harsh and tight. 'I asked Headquarters to confirm the finding of the court which tried you two weeks ago. In their wisdom – or their folly – they have decided not to confirm this. They have decided that there is a lack of real evidence here to enable the death sentence for treason to be carried out. I must say that I do not agree with this. To my mind, the charge was proved conclusively, without the slightest shadow of doubt.

'However, you have been found guilty of cowardice in the face of the enemy. I'm sure that this is a name which is going to stick to you for the rest of your life, even when the Army has finished with you. It's something indelible, which can't be rubbed off. You are no longer a commissioned officer. You will be stripped of all your insignia, reduced through the ranks to that of private and subjected to any further disciplinary action which I deem to be necessary. Do you have anything at all to say in view of this?'

Brad Calder drew himself tautly erect. A little of the

situation was now beginning to penetrate his curiously numbed mind. He knew instinctively that something was expected of him, yet could not think what it was. Colonel Weekes watched him closely, expectantly.

With an effort he cleared his throat. 'I've already said all there is to say, Colonel. I told the truth. There is a traitor here and accusing me of it, will not stop him. But nine men died out there in that wood and it's up to me to see that they are avenged. There will be a time when I can do that and this man, whoever he is, will die. Make no mistake about that.'

For a long moment the other stared up at him in the dim light inside the tent. He said: 'You know, Calder, I almost believe you. But the evidence is, to my mind, too overwhelming.'

There was no point in argument. Everything which had been said was done, finished with; and there were none of the men who had ridden out with him who could testify on his behalf. He was caught in a web of someone else's weaving and for the time being, could see no way out of it.

He stood quiet, motionless, looking down at the iron-grey hair of the Colonel, at the lined face which carried all of the weariness, the responsibility for the regiment. The worst thing of all, he thought, as he stood there, was that deep in his heart, Colonel Weekes really believed that he was doing what was right, really believed in his guilt. In a way, it was this that hurt more than anything else. It was then that he began to think about Captain Frye, the only other man who had known of those secret orders. It was something he was to think about for many years after that late evening, when he stood in front of Colonel Weekes, somewhere south of the Wilderness, where they were fighting a losing battle against the forces of the North.

2

VENGEANCE TRAIL

It was still early in the year, with the first growth of spring having already thrust its way through the dusty plains, but with full summer still some way ahead, the quiet, easy spell which lasted between the beginning of life for a new year and the lazy days of high summer, full of heat and dust. The man rode his mount slowly over the long rise which looked down on to the wide valley, watching everything with a keen eye, hearing all there was to be heard in this great wide wilderness with an attentive ear. It was something which had been with him for almost as long as he could remember, all the way from the south where the Badlands bordered on the southern lands of New Mexico.

The horse crossed the lip of a narrow gulch, paused as the earth gave under its questing hooves, then moved swiftly forward to firmer ground. Brad Calder sat hunched in his saddle, to ease the weight on his mount, pushed his hat over his forehead to shield his eyes from the savage sunglare. Ahead of him rose a bank of low hills, still several miles away, but rounded and inviting, shining in the harsh sunlight, beckoning him onward, promising him shade and coolness. Here, there was only the wide prairie, an open range of scrub and mesquite, thorn and stunted bushes, a place where a man could ride for days on end and be alone all the time.

Mid-afternoon, with the sun just leaving its zenith, with the heat-head lifted to its highest point of intensity, he reached a narrow creek that ran alongside the dim, dusty trail. Somewhere it would join a river, a river whose name he did not know. Sliding to the ground, he loosened the cinch and let the bay nibble at the short, tough grass which grew in profusion along the bank of the creek where the water had soaked through the earth. Roots had been put down here and everywhere there was evidence of growing things. It could be good land this, he thought idly, as he sat on his haunches, not moving, not hungry, building himself a cigarette. As he sat and smoked, the sunlight hot on his back and shoulders, he stared at the mountains in the far distance, then lowered his glance a little towards the nearer hills. Somewhere close by there had to be a town of some kind, no matter how small. He had heard at various points along the long trail from the south of the townships which were springing up in this territory now that the Civil War was over and the Indians had been driven out, put into the reservations where they could be watched closely. The frontier was being pushed west at an ever-increasing rate and wherever the ground was favourable, a town would be started. He had passed through one or two of them on his journey, a single dusty street that ran arrow-straight between low-roofed, single-storeyed houses, mostly of wood, the boardwalks of slatted pine. These towns were born; none of them, it seemed, had been planned. Hard men had built them, throwing up the log houses around a central nucleus, building with guts and sweat, giving everything they had so that they could spread their new civilization all the way across a continent.

He had stayed only briefly at any of these towns. There are few men who might still remember him, but he knew that the brand of coward would still cling to him, would remain associated with his name and his face until he had found the man who had ruined him, the man who had given that vital information to the enemy and left him to shoulder the blame. Whoever he was, it was not his fault that the death penalty had not been carried out. Only the fact that some man, nameless, faceless, at Headquarters, had decided there was not sufficient evidence to justify executing him in front of a firing squad, had saved him from death.

Deliberately, as he smoked, drawing the sweet smoke deeply into his lungs, letting it go through his nostrils, he shut his mind against the consuming anger that poured through him. There was no time for that right now. Since he had been released he had sought Captain Frye, feeling certain that even if the other were not the man he wanted, he knew something which could help him. But it had not been an easy task. The fighting had been long and bitter, casualties had been grievous on both sides. Colonel Weekes was somewhere in Washington now. Frye seemed to have dropped out of sight, until that day when he had ridden through a small town down near the Mexican frontier. He had raised a smell of the other there. Patient questioning had revealed that a man answering Frye's description had been there on three occasions during the past two years, buying cattle. No one knew here he stayed, except that it was north someplace, that he had a large ranch now, with several thousand head of cattle, was considered to be a rich and very influential man.

The news had come only partially as a surprise to Calder. He had known the other slightly during the fighting in the Wilderness, around Rapidan, knew a little of the other's background. Certainly his family did not have as much money as would be needed to set up a man to this extent. Yet where had Frye, if indeed it were him, got all of the money needed to start a ranch of his size? The obvious answer was that the North had paid their spies well during the fighting; and it was this idea which had been in his mind all the way from the south.

When he got to his feet and moved forward to tighten the cinch once more, the sunlight struck him full on the face, harsh and glaring. He flicked the cigarette away, climbed up into the saddle and remained there for a moment while he looked about him, the leather of the reins threaded through his fingers.

To anyone who had known him during the early part of the war, all those long, weary years before, there would have seemed little change in his outward appearance except for a few added wrinkles on his lean features, the fact that his skin was now burned a deeper shade of brown from the long exposure to the hot southern sun, and the wide-set eyes were a little deeper sunk in his head. But a closer examination would have revealed other changes. There was a harsh, almost fanatical set to his jaw, a flickering brightness in the depths of his eyes and they now had a way of looking at you as if they were staring right through you and not seeing the outer flesh at all.

There were many things which had come to this man who had been branded a coward; things a man learns only in war, or in a cell, isolated with his own thoughts, his own deep bitterness. For he had grown bitter. Now there was the determination in him that if the world wished to be evil and full of injustice, then that was the way he would be and those were the weapons he would use to fight it.

Now the war was over. There had been a pardon for many of the prisoners kept on a charge similar to his own. They had been men who had seen just one comrade too many die beside them, had heard one too many rifle shots, or had reached a point of mental pressure where something had had to give. In fighting like that, harsh and bitter, protracted and full of tiny, seemingly isolated incidents, the Army tended to forget the occasions when a man showed himself to be a hero, and remembered only the one instant when he was shown to be a coward. If looked at objectively, with everything weighed in the balance, his deeds of bravery must surely outmatch the one instance when he had run in the face of the enemy. But the Army did not do that, the Army could not forgive the one event in a thousand.

Kneeing the bay, he touched spurs to its flanks, urged it out of the shallow depression where the creek had gouged dirt from the ground in its onward rush to meet the river, and headed north, with the fiery disc of the sun gradually working its way around on his left, lowering towards the humped western horizon.

Later, when the sun touched the horizon, paused there for a moment, before dipping out of sight in a vast, soundless explosion of red and crimson, he reined the bay and made camp in a sandy depression, an arroyo that was deep enough to shelter him from most of the night wind which, at this time of the year, could be icy cold and where the fire he built would be hidden from the coyotes or prairie dogs. He had little fear of men spotting his camp. He had ridden for five days now without seeing a solitary rider along the trail and before that, he had spotted them only as smoke-clouds near the distant horizons, cutting their own trails across the plains; tracks criss-crossing over the great, dreaming face of this vast continent, with distances too wide for many of them to meet except where they came to one of the new towns which were springing up.

Dragging the saddle from the horse, he set it down on the ground, hobbled the bay a few yards away, then hunted around for brush and sun-dried twigs. There was plenty of twisted cirio wood around and after he had settled, he watched the sky over to the west change to pale blue and a copper-flame green. By the time the first bright stars were beginning to show overhead he was frying the last of his pork, listening to it sizzle in the pan, with the coffee bubbling over the flames.

All at once the greens and blues died, faded through a swift, transient indigo, and then it was dark. The air was cold now. The ground seemed anxious to give up all of the heat it had soaked up from the sun during the daytime, in the shortest possible time. He shivered as the coolness struck at his back, stretched out his hands to the flames.

There was the harsh, eerie wail of a coyote from somewhere close by. It was answered a few moments later, from a different direction. The shiver along his back increased, was due now to something more than the cold. There was something about that ghostly undulating wail that a man never got used to, no matter how often he heard it. There were other night noises that he recognized at once. The scurrying rush of a jackrabbit as it moved through the brush beyond the arroyo. The whirring of crickets sounded, faded, and then rose to another rasping crescendo.

He finished his meal, sat with his back to the earth wall of the arroyo. Starlight laid a faintly shimmering glow over everything. A night-owl hooted, low and soft, the echoes chasing each other across the flat plain. Lighting a smoke, he enjoyed it, drawing deeply on the cigarette, watching the blaze of the flames as they crept along the twigs and cino wood. The bay nickered softly, settling down for the night.

An hour before dawn, he was awake. He lay quite still under his blanket, straining to pick out any sound in the deathly, churchlike stillness that hung over the arroyo. His horse was standing with a patient quietness where he had left it. Carefully, he lifted himself on to his hands and knees, stood so that he could look over the crumbling rim of the arroyo. For a long period he could see nothing in the dimness. There was a moon, a yellow scratch in the sky, swinging low, close to the eastern horizon, giving little light. Then, as he peered out, trying to push his sight through the darkness which came shortly before the dawn, he heard the sharp break of gunfire away to the north. Shots came down to him on the little wind that blew over the range, making tiny, individual sounds in the air. He was in the arroyo, trapped there if any men were close by, could not move out without exposing himself on the skyline. He remained standing close to the rocky wall, debating the situation. The firing in the distance stayed brisk, coming now and then in louder volleys that cracked down over the ground and once, he thought he caught, above the sound of gunfire, the rumble of on-coming horses, headed in his direction.

A little later, he was sure. The steady abrasion of hoof-beats grew louder, on some other trail that ran at an angle to that on which he had been travelling. A faint movement at the very edge of vision, and he caught a glimpse of the grey cloud of dust lifted by a tight bunch of riders cutting across the skyline about a mile from him. The sound of their passage reached a peak and then began to die as they swung away from him. The men were pushing hard against the low hills.

Turning back to the fire, he kicked dirt over the last few glowing embers, stamped on them, then threw the saddle over the horse's back, made ready, and pulled himself up into the saddle. Once out of the arroyo, he rode steadily north, every sense alert. There was an emptiness and a strangely suppressed quiet that ate at his nerves like acid. The tiny spot in the middle of his back began to itch and he expected a shot from any direction with every passing second.

He was three miles from the spot where he had made camp for the night and had urged his horse on when it showed signs of slackening its pace. He was in the notch of a narrow, steep-sided canyon, with the rocky walls closing in on him from both sides when he heard the firing start up once more. It made only a brief sound to disturb the stillness, but it added to his apprehension and his hand hovered close to the butt of his revolver as he rode forward anxious to be out of the canyon and in more open ground, knowing that he would have no place in which to manoeuvre if he were caught here. His military training came back to him, urging him to move more quickly, but commonsense warned him that to do so could be dangerous, could give away his presence there. At the moment he was not sure what he had to be afraid of, but he had no wish to ride into the middle of a range war with his eyes shut.

The horse moved into a dispirited run, hooves kicking with a metallic sound against the hard, rocky floor of the canyon. Ahead of him, ragged and saw-toothed, the canyon walls began to dip downward. There was a sharply-angled bend in the trail and he slowed his mount as he approached it. Some instinct warned him that there might be trouble lying in wait for him just around this bend, yet when it came it was with the stunning shock of the totally unexpected.

The rifle shot came from behind one of the high boulders overlooking the trail to his right. The bullet hit the ground less than three feet from him, went whining off into the distance in murderous ricochet. A hard voice yelled: 'Hold it right there, mister.'

His first impulse was to wheel his mount around, cut back into the canyon, make a stand there. But he fought it down at once, knowing he hadn't the ghost of a chance of making it before collecting a bullet in the back. Whoever was up there had a high-powered rifle and he knew how to use it, was obviously something of a marksman, even in that poor light. For had that bullet been so intended, it would certainly have knocked him out of his saddle, pitching him to the ground, with that tiny piece of lead lodged in his heart or brain.

He felt the cold anger burning deeply in him, but forced himself to relax, lifting his hands slowly until they were above shoulder level. 'All right,' he called, after a few moments of uneasy silence, 'what is this: a hold-up?'

'Keep your hands where they are,' called the voice once more.

He turned his head slowly, trying to pick out where the other was, but in the dimness and with the rocks picking up the echoes and flinging them in all directions, it was just not possible to judge with any accuracy where the hidden gunman was. A moment later a shadow moved on the opposite side of the canyon. Loose rocks slid down the rocky face and bounced across the uneven floor of the canyon. The shadow came forward until the man was level with him, putting up a hand to take the Winchester from its scabbard and tossing it into the tumbled boulders that lay alongside the trail.

'Now lift out your Colts, slow and easy,' murmured a harsh voice.

Brad obeyed. It was a galling thing to have to do but in the circumstances he had no other choice. Slowly, he lifted the Colts from their holsters with his thumb and forefinger and let them drop.

With a barely-controlled anger, Brad said softly, very soft: 'I said before and I'll say it again: What is this?'

'You'll see,' snarled the man beside him. 'Get down off that horse – and hurry!'

He slid to the ground, stood looking across at the other. The man was short and squat, with broad, square shoulders, a face that seemed slablike, as if chipped from a block of granite, eyes that stared out at him from beneath thick, lowered brows. The other's companion came sliding down the rocks, the rifle held in his right hand.

'He could be one of them,' murmured the man with the rifle. He walked around Calder's horse, examining it closely. 'No brand here but they wouldn't be so foolish as to do that just in case we dropped one of 'em and got his horse. That would be the proof we needed.'

'Should there be a brand?' Brad asked. 'Just what are you gettin' at?'

'You don't know?' snapped the short man. He glared at Brad. 'Where are you from?'

'North Texas.'

'Can you prove that?'

Brad narrowed his eyes. He shook his head. 'There ain't any way I can prove it,' he said thinly; 'you know that.'

'Then where are you headed?'

'I'm looking for a man,' he said tightly. 'I've been looking for him for a long time.'

The two men exchanged brief glances. 'And when you find this man?'

A pause, then: 'I shall kill him and that will be the end of it.'

'So? You're a man who's ridin' a vengeance trail.' The short man drew back his lips, revealing his teeth. 'Sometimes you can get caught up in somethin' a heap bigger than what you set out to do.'

'I don't understand. I've never seen either of you two men before and —'

'I think you're lyin', mister. I think you're one of that bunch who tried to hit the herd an hour ago. We lost a handful of men in that sneak attack and I reckon it would be proper justice if we was to show those critters that they can't hit us and get away with it.'

'I don't know what you're talking about.' Brad thinned his lips. 'Sure I heard shootin' a little while ago, saw a bunch of riders heading out to the hills, but I was in an arroyo then where I'd made night camp. I don't know who those men were.'

'Sure, sure.' nodded the other. 'You'd say anythin' now that we're here.' Brad could see in the faint, growing grey

light that the other was sweating. It lay in a palely-gleam-
ing mask on his face and his eyes were unnaturally bright.

He knew instinctively that the other would kill him if he
made any move, and he did not try. There was a tightness
under his ribs but he tried not to show it. 'All right,' he
said evenly, 'you've got me mixed up with somebody else.
I can't prove I'm not with these riders who you say
attacked your herd. I guess that it's stalemate.'

'Not quite, stranger,' grated the taller man. 'We're
goin' to give you somethin' that'll make not only you, but
the others, remember.'

Calder tensed as the two men stepped closer. He
looked quickly from one man to the other, then acted.
Savagely, stepping swiftly to the right, he feinted with his
left hand, swung hard with his right fist, felt a sense of
satisfaction as his knuckles connected with the short
man's face. The other staggered back under the force of
the blow, blood spurting from his nose. Brad moved to
follow up, turned to face the other man, saw that he had
stepped back, out of reach of Brad's swinging fists but
not so far that he could not use the rifle he held to its
best advantage. It swung high in the air, held tightly by
the end of the barrel. Brad saw it descending, tried to get
away from under it, but only partly succeeded. The stunning blow caught him on the shoulder, knocked him
sideways, off-balance. It was as though sudden paralysis
had struck him down one side. The strength ran out of
his left arm and shoulder, and a numbing agony shot
through them. He tried to breathe but it was as if his
lungs were crushed inside his chest, making it impossible
to get the much-needed air down into them. For a
second, he remained upright, unable to move, knowing
that another blow was on the way, yet not capable of
doing anything about it. This time, the butt of the rifle
hit him squarely on the side of the head. When he was on
his knees, unable to see or hear, the smaller man came

forward, eyes glittering. There was the click of the hammer of a gun being drawn back.

Brad heard it only faintly, yet knew what it was and instinctively, he braced himself for the smashing impact of the leaden bullet.

'No!' hissed the taller man. 'That is not the way for this one. It could be that he is tellin' the truth.'

'We can't afford to let him go now. He's seen us. He could recognize us again and —'

'Not if we make sure that he won't come back this way,' said the other, his tone very soft.

Brad opened his eyes, shaking his head a little in an effort to clear his vision and rid his head of the pounding ache at the back of his temples. He saw the braced legs of one of the men, planted firmly on the ground directly in front of him. Feebly, he tried to lunge forward, hands reaching out for them, seeking to hurl the other off balance. But the weakness in his body was too much for him and he half-slid, half-fell on to his face at the other's feet. A hand caught at the back of his jacket, twisted the cloth into a tight bunch, hauled him upright.

One side of his head was strangely numb, although a little of the feeling had been shocked back into his body. There was the sticky, crusty feeling of blood on his face, trickling down from below his ear. He stiffened to receive another blow, felt a fist smash into his ribs. His shirt ripped as he rolled on the needle-tipped rocks. The sounds he heard all seemed to be reaching him from some tremendous distance, making little sense, words all blurred and jumbled together, the syllables running into one another, forming a continual roar of sound.

The pain of hitting the ground jarred redly through him, spilling the air out of his lungs once again. He coughed and retched painfully. Something told him insistently that he had to remain conscious, that whatever happened, he must not let himself go. He tried to push himself up on to his knees but a boot lifted and kicked him squarely in the chest. Once more he was lying face downward on the hard, cold ground, his body a mass of bruises, a stabbing pain lancing through his chest whenever he tried to suck in a gulp of air. Maybe one or more of his ribs were broken. The thought raced once through his head and was then lost in the confused welter of half-formed ideas and brief flashes of pain. A foot grated on the loose gravel near his face. Once again he was lifted from the ground as the short man hissed: 'Hold him there, Abe, I'm goin' to give him a little treatment of my own, just to make sure he doesn't come round this way again. He's got to be made to remember this.'

More blows, on his arms and shoulders, on the side of his face until his cheek was on fire, grazed and bleeding. Hammer-like blows which bounced off his ribs until his chest was a mass of agony. He tried to open his mouth, to shout a protest, that he was not the man they clearly seemed to think he was, but no words came out and the harsh croaking sounds were unintelligible.

Finally, they stopped their beating. Standing back, their own breathing, hard and loud, lifting on the stillness, their hands and arms hanging limply by their sides, they watched him as he lay on the stony ground, in the first grey flush of dawn.

'Do we leave his horse?' asked the tall man tautly.

The other considered it, then nodded. 'I guess so. He'll know better than to try to follow us. Reckon he'll head north. We'll see if they take care of him. When they know we caught him, they may think twice about tryin' to hit us again.'

'Reckon we can take these with us.' The other picked up the guns and the rifle from where they had fallen. 'Guess he won't be wantin' them.' He grinned viciously. Sucking his knuckles, he walked along the canyon to where their horses were tethered, stood waiting for the other.

For a moment, the short man waited, staring down at the unconscious man on the canyon floor, then he spun on his heels and joined his companion. Climbing into the saddle, they rode off to the east and soon there was a deep grey silence closing in on the canyon and only the bay moved as it waited and became impatient in the dawn light.

The heat, blazing down on his back, finally brought him to consciousness. It was a painful return to sensibility. For a long period he lay there, sprawled on his face, unable to move, even to ease the blistering heat on his torn and bruised back. His arms were like lead with no feeling whatever in them and whenever he tried to open his eyes and keep them open the savage glare, reflected from the smooth rock of the sheer wall in front of him, forced him to close them again, although there still remained a coppery glare on the inner surface of his eyelids, glancing into his brain.

There was a period when time had no meaning at all, when he seemed to exist in some strange hiatus, hovering between consciousness and unconsciousness. His tunic had been ripped off him and his shirt torn to tattered ribbons, exposing his back to the full glare of the sun.

At last, making a supreme effort, he was able to keep his eyes open and to force himself over on one elbow. There was no cloud in the sky and no shade for him anywhere now that the sun was fast approaching its zenith. Sucking in a deep breath, even though it hurt his chest to do so, he forced his vision through the stabbing glare until he was able to pick out the shape of the bay, standing a few yards away at the head of the canyon. He let his breath go in a long sigh.

At least, there was still a chance for him if only he could somehow get up into the saddle and stay there. It was not going to be easy. There was scarcely any strength left in his body and even the slightest movement was sufficient to send agony lancing through his limbs, bringing the sweat boiling out on his forehead and back. Overhead, he noticed, a small flock of buzzards, tattered strips of black cloth, sailed in lazy circles in the strong sunlight. They sensed a kill, would swoop lower if he did not make a move. Gritting his teeth he finally succeeded in pushing himself up on to his knees, rested there for several minutes, as needle-sharp pinpricks of fire stabbed at his arms and legs with returning feeling. The numbness went slowly away to be replaced by an agony that was somehow even worse. But he told himself that if he did not move now he never would; thought about Frye, the man he was seeking, and the saving anger boiled up inside him. giving him the desperate strength he needed.

Clinging to the rough wall of the canyon, he staggered towards the waiting horse. It shied away a little as he drew nearer to it, not recognizing him and he called softly to it, his voice little more than a harsh croak, rasping in his parched throat. The horse stopped, remained where it was as he stumbled towards it.

Around him the rocky walls of the canyon reeled and dipped in front of his aching, straining vision. Several times he fell, lay for long moments while he summoned sufficient strength to continue, clawing his way upright; fingers torn and bleeding on the stones. When he finally reached the bay, he lacked the strength to climb up into the saddle. His legs were like water, his knees giving under him. The burning dust was in his mouth and on his lips, stinging his eyes as it worked its way under the lids. The resin breath of the distant hills came in to him on a little wind that sighed over the canyon, making its way over the gullies nearby.

'Down, horse,' he said croakingly. The animal recognized his voice, moved closer, bending and nuzzling at him. It smelled the dried blood and backed away in momentary alarm, then came forward again, a little surer of him this time. He sucked in a gust of air, felt his ribs burn under the flesh, waited until the savage stabbing pain had eased, then caught at the horse's fetlock, pulled with all of his strength until the animal was forced down on to its forelegs. It stayed there while he eased one leg up into the stirrup. Pain was a suffusing ache in him, every movement, however slight, an eternity of agony. But at last he made it, clinging on to the reigns with bleeding fingers. The bay lifted itself gently, seeming to understand what was wrong, got to its feet and with Brad lying almost on his face across its back began the slow, steady walk towards the hills on the skyline.

Somehow they made it. Several times Brad hovered dangerously close to the limit of consciousness, feeling his senses slip from him, sensing the blackness closing in on him from all sides. Yet with a supreme effort, he managed to stay in the saddle, sweat boiling from his forehead, mingling with the blood and dust on his face, trickling in irritating streams down the folds of skin on his cheeks.

The bay continued into the timber where a narrow road came in from the surrounding desert to the east, cut over a river by means of a log bridge and so entered the tall pines. The horse came to a trembling halt by the bank of the river after moving slowly over the bridge. Dimly, Brad was aware of the sound of running water and when the bay did not move again, he somehow slid from the saddle, hit the ground hard, lost consciousness for several minutes.

When he came round he was awake in a great green dimness and gradually his eyes focused on points of light, harsh and glaring and he knew that it was the sunlight streaming down through gaps in the leafy canopy overhead. There was a numbness in his left side and when he tried to move, darting pains laced through his arm and ribs and the agony warned him not to move too much.

Carefully, he moved his head with a wrenching of neck muscles, trying to make out the cause of the dull roaring in his ears. Then he saw the water cascading past his face less than six inches away and somehow managed to heave his body over the smooth grass until he could lower his head and let the water ripple over his torn flesh, stinging where it touched the wounds and bruises, but refreshing, shocking some of the life back into his body and numbed mind.

An hour passed; and then another. Even under the trees, some of the heat managed to get through and he lay there on the cool grass, soaking it up, letting it pour into his body, the bay cropping quietly beside him. At last, he dragged himself upright, washed some of the caked blood from his arms and chest, drank of the cold water until he could hold no more.

He knew that he was still badly hurt, that his injuries needed tending, but he could think clearly now and the threat of unconsciousness seemed to have receded. He tested himself by forcing himself to his feet, stood there swaying as the blood rushed, pounding sickly, to his head. But he managed to remain upright. Pulling himself up into the saddle, he took the trail through the high timber, still heading north, came out into more open country and in the distance, perhaps two miles away, it widened to more than six times its present size and formed the main street of a small town, a cluster of buildings built along either side of the street. There was timber on three sides of the town, growing close as if grudging it the right to be there while on the fourth side, to the north, the trail lifted steeply towards a high ridge that dominated the whole scene.

As yet, he did not even know the name of this town, but he had guessed there would be a place somewhere around and this was as likely a spot as anywhere he could get some help for his injuries. The Sheriff, too, might know of the two men who had jumped him.

He rode slowly into the town, the tired hoofs of his bay striking a muffled tattoo on the dry dust of the street. Immediate concern being some attention for the cuts and bruises, the possibly cracked ribs in his chest, he headed for the feed stable and corral, found it a little off the main street and as he passed through the town, although aware of the curious stares at his appearance, he made a guarded survey of the place. On the face of things it looked like one more cowtown along this frontier, no better and no worse than a score of others he had seen since leaving Texas. He noticed the way the idle talk among the men on the boardwalk ceased as he drew level with them, only to continue once he had ridden past. It was, he reflected, something of an uneasy town; and that fitted in with what had happened to him and what little he had gained from the two men who had jumped him in the canyon. There was a range war in the making here, possibly with two open powder kegs lying around, rancher against rancher, or rancher against nester, and it would need only one spark to set the entire range ablaze.

At the entrance to the shadowy stables, a roustabout appeared, eyed him with a surly glance, then looked down at the horse.

'It'll cost you half a dollar for a manger of hay, a stall and a feed of oats,' he said, speaking through his teeth.

Brad nodded, slid from the saddle, gritting his teeth as pain jarred along his legs and up into his body. 'Fair enough,' he acknowledged. 'Make it a generous helping of oats. It's been a hard ride.'

The other took the reins from him. 'You look as if you've been in a fight yourself, Mister,' he muttered.

'Something like that,' Brad agreed. His voice was bleak. 'You know where I can find the Sheriff?'

The other glanced at him for a moment, then said: 'Should be in his office right now. Hansett don't usually go over to the saloon much before sundown.'

'Thanks.' Brad nodded, gave the other the half dollar, then went out into the street, angled across it to where he saw the Sheriff's Office, hemmed in between the Bank and a storehouse.

Hansett was a burly, florid-faced man, with iron-grey hair and a bristle moustache. He gave Brad a casual nod, motioned him to the chair in front of the desk, but there was nothing casual in the glance which ran over the other, taking in everything about him.

'What can I do for you. Mister —?'

'Calder. Brad Calder.' He fingered his cheek for a moment, wincing a little. 'I was jumped by a couple of men along the trail at first light this morning. Seems they may have mistaken me for somebody else.'

The other dug in his pocket, pulled out a long cigar, bit the end off and spat it into the corner, then struck a sulphur match and applied the flame to the end of it, sucking deeply. 'You recognize either of these men again if you saw 'e, Mister Calder?'

'Sure. Both of them.'

The Sheriff stared down at the glowing tip of his cigar, then put his glance on Brad again. 'You seem mighty certain of that. You say it was first light. Reckon it couldn't have been easy to make them out too plainly.'

'It was easy enough,' Brad said coldly, his tone stiff. 'I was standing right up to them. Seems they reckoned I was riding with a bunch of men who attacked their herd. I did hear riders a little while before I ran into these two *hombres*. Woke me up where I'd made camp.'

'I see. And you weren't ridin' with these men?'

Brad said nothing for a moment. Here, he thought, was the veiled hostility and suspicion which he had encountered at times before among those who knew his name. He felt sure that no one here did, but evidently they did not like strangers riding into town and making accusations. It was, he decided there and then, about time he met this attitude head on.

'What're you trying to get at, Sheriff? You're supposed to be the law around here and when someone rides in with a complaint, it's up to you to investigate it. Seems to me you're trying your best to call me a liar, or something worse. I'm telling you I'd know both of those men again. They took my guns and rifle, beat me up. I aim to find out who they were and why they did that. Then, if the law does nothing, I'll decide what to do myself.'

'Now hold on there a minute, Mister Calder.' The other leaned forward, resting his elbows on the desk. 'You can't start tryin' to take the law into your own hands. If you try that, then I'll have to stop you.'

'All right then. Why don't you start doin' somethin' about it? You know who owns the big ranches in this part of the territory. You know if there's any kind of feud goin' on, any range war building up to explosion point. I figure you must have a good idea who those two men were, or at least who they work for.'

The Sheriff frowned. He seemed torn between two loyalties, Brad thought, eyeing him closely. It could be that the cattlemen had put him into office and if he wanted to remain at Sheriff, he had to do as he was told.

'You're right, there has been trouble lately. So far, it's been little more than skirmishes between bands of men out on the prairies. Nesters have tried to run off the cattle from the range and a couple of homesteads have been fired in return. But so far, it's nothin' we can't handle, so long as no new element comes along.'

'And you're thinking maybe, that I'm the new element you're afraid of.'

'Could be. You have the look of a man hellbent for trouble. Seems you've caught some of it already. And you won't stop until you've found these two men and called them out. That's the way of it, ain't it?'

'Let's say I don't think it's polite to beat up a perfect

stranger as they did. I'd never seen either of those men before in my life.' He sat back deeper in his chair as pain burned again at the back of his forehead. Reaching up, he wiped the thin film of sweat away with the sleeve of his torn jacket.

'You're in a bad way, Mister.' Hansett pushed himself up out of his chair and came around the side of the desk. 'Reckon I'd better get you over to Doc Horgan. Now just take things easy and he'll put you right in no time.'

Brad felt the faintness coming over him again, fought savagely against it, teeth pressed tightly together, the muscles of his jaw lumping painfully under the skin. The flesh on his back remained hot and agonizing as the Sheriff got an arm around him, helping him from the chair until he was able to stand upright. Curious eyes watched as Hansett helped him along the hollow-sound-ing boardwalk, paused in front of a door fifty yards from his office and rapped loudly.

A few moments later the door swung creakingly open. The man who stood there, his features wavering in front of Brad's stultified vision, was thin to the point of gauntness, flesh drawn down tight against the planes of his face.

'Give me a hand with him, Doc,' he heard Hansett say, his voice coming from a great distance, fading and approaching in a manner that was perplexing. 'He's been hurt bad somewhere along the trail.'

'Get him inside and I'll take a look at him.' Together, they half-carried him into the front room, laid him down on the long couch. Only vaguely, was he aware of what happened later. There were disconnected memories later, none making sense at the time, but most of the while, he was barely conscious.

'You any idea what happened to him Hansett?' asked Horgan as he fetched his instruments from the cupboard.

'Only what he told me in my office. Seems a couple of boys from the Lazy J spotted him heading along the trail shortly before dawn, must've figured he was one of the band of nesters who hit their herd during the night. They did a good job on him by the looks of things.'

'Too goddamned quick to use their fists and boots,' said the other through his teeth. He did not look at the Sheriff as he went on: 'Things are getting to the stage when somethin' will have to be done about the Lazy J hands. They're startin' too much trouble.'

'You can't blame 'em, Doc,' said the other, a trifle defensively. 'After all, this mob have been running off their beef for some time now. They got a right to protect those steers.'

'That don't allow them the right to beat up innocent men on the trail,' muttered the other as he bent over the man on the couch and began to strip off the tattered remains of his shirt, exposing the cuts and bruises on the man's back. 'You figuring on doin' anything about this?'

'I'll want to question this fella first,' said Hansett, after a brief pause. 'There's somethin' to his story that don't quite tie in. I ain't sure what it is at the moment, but I mean to find out before I ride out start accusin' those men. What's this *hombre* doin' here anyway? He says he's from Texas. That's the best part of seven hundred miles away. He must have a reason for ridin' that far.' Hansett stepped back a little, resting his shoulders against the wall, his thumbs hooked inside his gunbelt. He pushed out his lower lip. 'How bad is he hurt?'

'It's serious. Not that he's likely to die, but he's goin' to know that he's been beaten up.'

'I don't suppose it could've been an accident?'

Horgan looked up from washing the wounds, shook his head emphatically. 'Not a chance. He was beaten near dead, probably left to die. He must've found the river and washed some of the blood and dirt off. Could've lost quite a heap of blood too. Surprised, he managed to get here like he did.'

Hansett sighed audibly. 'They took his guns away too.' He moved away. 'I'll have a talk with him when he's on his feet again. How long's that likely to be?'

'Hard to say. He's evidently got a good strong constitution and that's going to help him. I'll keep him here until he's recovered a little.'

'You sure you can manage?'

'I'll manage. Janet Frye usually comes in to help me. She'll lend a hand, I'm sure.' He looked up sharply. 'You don't think those two *hombres* will trail him here to finish the job, do you?'

'It's not likely.' Hansett paused in the doorway, then gave a quick nod and left. A moment later the front door closed and there was the sound of the other's heavy tread on the boardwalk.

Doc Horgan waited for a moment, then went back to work, his skilful fingers moving over the torn body of the man lying on the couch. Several times the other moaned deep in his throat, stirred faintly as though coming out of the depths of unconsciousness. Once his eyes flickered open, rested on his face for a moment, but there was no sign of recognition in them, no awareness of his surroundings. The brief flicker of consciousness lasted for only a few seconds, then the other had slipped back again and Horgan waited for a moment, then turned him over on to his side, examining the bruised ribs.

Slowly, the pain in his side increased to the point where his awareness of it was greater than the shrouding blackness which had held him enmeshed for what seemed an eternity. He struggled to open his eyes. When he did so, light blazed against them and he squeezed them shut, screwing them up as stabs of agony lanced into his skull. Keeping them shut, he began to move his body, slowly and experimentally. Something was wrapped tightly around his chest and it made it difficult for him to draw in a deep breath.

He knew he had to open his eyes to see what had happened to him.

The pain was still there when he opened them again, turning his head a little to shield his eyes from the searing glare of sunlight. Wincing a little, he lifted himself up on to his elbows. At the same moment, he became aware that he was not alone in the room. The door had opened quietly and someone had stepped inside, coming up to the foot of the bed, looking down at him. Squinting against the light, he saw the girl standing there, resting her hands on the footboard. She had a clear, honest face, open and frank, framed by dark hair which fell in smooth waves to her shoulders.

She nodded without speaking, then turned away and went over to the far side of the room, picked up a tray, and brought it over to him.

He licked his lips a little, tasted salt on them, said: 'I'm not hungry, thanks.'

She took the cover from the tray, set it down in front of him. 'That's no excuse for not eating,' she said softly, her voice low. 'You've been very ill, and now you have to start building up your strength again – or would you rather that I called the doctor and got him to make you eat something?'

He hesitated, then shook his head. 'All right, Ma'am. Where is this place, by the way?'

'This is Dr Horgan's house. He took you in when the Sheriff brought you over. You'd been beaten up pretty badly.'

'When was that?'

'Day before yesterday. Sometime in the afternoon, I think. Don't you remember anything about it?'

He rubbed his forehead with his fingertips. Then he shook his head a little. 'Funny, I don't seem to recall anything clearly. I remember two men stopping me in a canyon somewhere out on the trail, getting me mixed up with somebody and beating me up. After that, there seems to be only snatches. This is a town, isn't it?'

'That's right. This is Medicine Reach.' Her forehead creased with tiny lines of puzzlement. 'Sheriff Hansett said you told him you were from Texas. That's a long way.'

'I'm looking for a man, Miss —'

'Frye,' she said simply. 'I'm Janet Frye.'

3

LAZY J

Brad heard the girl's words as if in a deep, muffling silence. But only a faint, twitching of a tiny muscle high in his cheek betrayed anything he might have been feeling inwardly. He ate the food mechanically, chewing over each mouthful before swallowing it. The soup was hot with pieces of meat floating in it and it brought a little strength back into his body, a little strength into his arms and legs.

'Who were the men who did this to you?' Janet Frye asked, after a long pause.

'I don't know. I never saw them before. They work for one of the big ranches here, I think. I heard them say they figured I was ridin' with a bunch of men who had tried to rustle cattle that night.'

For a moment he saw a faint gust of expression go over her features, then it was gone and he could not be sure what it had been. Fear, realization? It was impossible to tell.

'Sheriff Hansett wants to ask you some more questions as soon as you feel fit enough. Doc Horgan was worried about you at first. Said you'd lost a great deal of blood,

55

didn't know how you had managed to stay alive all the way into town.'

He smiled thinly at that remark. 'When a man has the thought of vengeance on his mind, it takes a lot to finish him.'

'I thought that might be one of the reasons you came here,' she said simply. 'But I was hoping that it wasn't.'

'You think a man should forget what is done to him, let it pass as if nothing has happened?'

'I think a man should be forgiving,' she said after a pause.

He looked up sharply. He felt entitled to be both angry and desirous of revenge, not only on the man who had branded him a coward all those years before, but now on the two men who had beaten him in this way. He had always believed that some degree of anger inside a man was a good thing, it could drive him on to do things which otherwise he would never dare to do. The frontiers of this country would never have been pushed back westward had it not been for men who were angry, dissatisfied with their lot back east, determined to beat this new land which lay west of the great cities, to shape it into something new and vital.

'How's my horse?' he asked, changing the subject adroitly. 'I left it over the street at the stable.'

'He's being taken care of,' she said promptly. 'The groom remembered you when you rode in.'

'Good. If it hadn't been for him I'd probably have died out there. He deserves the best there is.'

She stretched forward and took the empty plate away. 'The Sheriff will be coming in a few minutes. Maybe you'd better get a little rest until he gets here. You're still very weak.'

He lay back in the bed as she left the room, closing the door gently behind her. His chest had been strapped up tightly. Probably a couple of broken ribs, he thought. But most of the dizziness seemed to have left him and he was able to think more clearly now, to put little disconnected thoughts together in his mind, to form some idea of what had happened, casting his mind back, dragging brief memories out of the dark blankness which had earlier engulfed him. Dominating everything was the shock he had felt when the girl had told him her name. It could have been coincidence, but somehow he did not think so; and that vague look on her face when he had mentioned the two men as having been working for some big ranch in the territory. Alarm, perhaps? He rolled his weight on the bed, easing his body from side to side, silently struggled through the pain of the cracked ribs.

A few moments later the door opened and the Sheriff came inside. He nodded a brief greeting. Behind him came a thin-faced man he guessed to be the doctor.

'Feeling better, Calder?' asked Hansett, taking his ease in one of the tall, leather-backed chairs. 'If you feel up to answerin' some of my questions, I'd like to have a little talk with you.'

'I'll tell you anything I can,' Brad said slowly. He eyed the other shrewdly.

'Suppose that you tell us all about it, from the beginning. Why you rode here from Texas in the first place. What you've got on your mind. What is it, Calder? Revenge, vengeance?'

'Maybe I've got a score to settle,' Brad said easily. 'That's probably the reason I came here. It has nothing to do with what happened out there on the trail. Nothing at all.'

Hansett lifted his thick brows momentarily, regarded Brad in silence for a second. He leaned back in the chair until the leather creaked in protest, crossed his legs. 'All right, so you won't tell us about that. Let's hear about these two men who stopped you and beat you. They could have killed you more easily than beating you half to death. Why didn't they?'

'How should I know? Maybe they figured I'd set an example to those rustlers they thought I belonged to. A dead man means nothing. But a man beaten up is something they can see in front of them for a long time, a constant reminder. Besides, they probably know you'd have to get a posse together and go looking for them if they'd shot me down in cold blood after taking my guns.'

'That's a fair answer. Could be that's the way they had it figured. But if I should find them, I'll need you to identify them. Where will you be once you got back on your feet?'

'He can come out and stay at the Lazy J ranch,' said a voice from the doorway. Brad turned his head swiftly, saw Janet Frye standing there. She smiled warmly at him.

He bit his lower lip, then shook his head. 'I couldn't do that,' he said, quickly.

'But why not? We need men. I'm sure you can handle cattle as well as the next man and you don't have the look of one of the nesters who are trying to move into the territory.'

'I'm not a nester,' he said; 'but I can't impose on your generosity like this. Besides, I have a lot of business here in town. It might take me quite a while to get it finished.'

'You'll be safer on the ranch.' There was a curiously strained inflection to her tone. He saw her glance slide from the doctor's face to that of the Sheriff. 'Medicine Reach has the reputation of being an uneasy sort of town.'

'I've had it figured for that,' he nodded. 'And thanks for the offer. If I can get my business finished, I might like to take it up then.'

'All right.' She nodded her head but the smile did not come back. 'I hope, for your sake, that you've made the right decision.'

She turned and went out. Sheriff Hansett said: 'Guess you touched a sore point there, young fella. Her Dad owns the biggest ranch in these parts. But since this trouble with the nesters, things have been goin' against them and they look on strangers as taking sides. If you aren't for them, then they consider you're with the nesters.'

'And if you don't take either side?'

'They reckon that ain't possible after you've been here for a while.' His tone sobered. 'I figure you ought to walk real careful in Medicine Reach when you get back on to your feet and start moving around again. As for this man you're huntin', if he's here and on either side, be doubly careful. A bullet can come from any shadow after dark.'

It was two weeks before he got out of that room. At the end of another five days he went out into the main street of the town. The middle-morning sun touched him warmly, soaking through the clean shirt he wore, into the healing flesh of his back. His ribs were almost completely healed now and there was only a vague ache in his chest whenever he pressed the spot.

After checking on his mount he made his way across to the hotel. It was a weather-beaten place of two storeys, standing head and shoulders above the low, wooden buildings on either side. All across the front of it ran a galleried porch, the top of which forced a balcony for the upper rooms. The lobby was plainly furnished, but clean and well-swept and the clerk who eyed him curiously for a moment from behind the desk, chewed on a long cigar, the smoke curling up around his weasel-like features. The eyebrows drew close together when he noticed who it was. He said stiffly: 'Ain't you the *hombre* who rode into town three weeks ago and got taken across to Doc Horgan's place?'

'That's right.' Here, thought Brad, was the animosity again, the thinly veiled distrust and hostility. He began to wonder if there might not be something more to it than he saw on the surface. It was a thing he had noticed at once, that day he had first ridden into this town. Then he had thought that it might have been connected in some way with his appearance, but now he felt that this was not the case.

'You got a room here?'

The other chewed on the end of the cigar for a moment, twisting it around his thin lips before answering. The casualness with which he spoke was too disinterested to be entirely convincing. 'We've got a room, sure. You got any money?'

In answer Brad tossed a couple of coins on to the top of the desk. 'These should take care of it for a while. If I decide to stay any longer, I'll let you know.'

The man took the cigar from his mouth, glanced at the smoking tip for a moment, then shrugged his shoulders and spun the register, handing the pen across to him. Brad signed his name with a flourish. The clerk studied the signature for a second, then turned and took a key down from the rack on the wall behind him. 'Room Seven. At the end of the corridor, top of the stairs.' He pointed. 'Breakfast at seven, dinner at one, and supper at seven. That suit you?'

'It suits me fine,' Brad said. He made his way up the narrow, creaking stairs, along the corridor at the top and unlocked the door of the room at the far end. Going inside, he turned and locked the door behind him, then looked around. The room was plainly furnished like the lobby with an iron bed in one corner, the sheets clean, a thin, threadbare carpet in front of the window where it looked out on to the balcony and further, across the roofs of the other buildings, out to where the ground rose steeply towards the hills which dominated that side of the town. In the other direction, he could see the thick timber, pressing close against the outskirts. Making himself a smoke, he lit it carefully, let a thin line of pale blue smoke curl up from his lips and sat down in the high-backed chair near the wash-stand.

Sitting there he allowed his thoughts to go back over the days and weeks since he had ridden out of his home state to come north, seeking the man who had either been the traitor to the Confederate Cause, or who would give him the information which could lead him to that man. Now, by force of circumstance, here he was in this tiny township of Medicine Reach, faced with the fact that the girl who had helped him, who had watched over him while his injuries had slowly healed, was perhaps related to the Captain Frye he was seeking. On the other hand, he could not, as yet, be absolutely certain that the rancher who owned the Lazy J was the same man. This, he reflected, could turn out to be the meanest chore he had ever undertaken. Plainly, the hills around here were renegade country, would harbour men on the dodge, men who were running from the law, hunted ones, their faces on the wanted posters scattered across the whole state, men with prices on their heads. They, no doubt, would prey on cattleman and nester alike. They were the men on the outer fringe, men for whom constant wariness and a distrust of all other men, was the only guarantee of their continued freedom.

It was doubtful if he could get any information from the ranchers, or the hired hands who worked for them. The nesters might provide him with information, but they too would be wary of someone who was so obviously a cattleman. That left the renegades, the wanted men, and getting news from them, as from one man to another, could turn out to be a very dangerous chore. As he had been warned already, a shot or a knife could, so easily, come from the darkness . . .

He pushed himself to his feet, stubbed out the butt of the cigarette in the small tray and wiped the grey ash from his fingers. Down below, in the street, hoofbeats sounded hollowly on the dry dust and he went over to the window, peering out. Two riders were leaving town, moving fast,

kicking up spurts of dust behind them. He did not recognize any of the men but he noticed the way in which they
rode, saw another small group of men turning away from
the hitching rail of one of the saloons a little further down
the street, where they had obviously been in recent
conversation with the two riders, noticed their vehement
talk and gestures as they went inside the saloon, letting the
batwing doors swing shut behind them. His lips thinned
back in a faint smile of ironic amusement. He did not
doubt that they had been discussing him. Since he had
ridden into town, he would have been talked about, his
motives for being there analysed. Frowning with specula-
tive thought, he sank back on to the chair again, hands
clasped behind his neck, trying to think things out in his
mind.

The naked hostility in this town was something he had
not expected to find. He was a stranger here yet they all
seemed to have decided that he was trouble four ways
come Sunday. Did they usually pre-judge a man like this?
Or was there something more ominous at the back of it?
The more he thought about it, the more convinced he was
that this was the answer; yet he could not see what it could
be.

Presently, he shrugged, settled his body more comfort-
ably in the chair and closed his eyes. He must have dozed
off, although he had not intended to do so, for when he
woke, there was the sound of the supper gong resonating
from somewhere down the stairs. Yawning, he got to his
feet. He had not realized that he had been asleep for so
long. But when he stepped across to the window he saw
that the sun had lowered itself down towards the tall hill to
the north and was now almost hidden in a smoky purple
mist and on the crests of them, a red flush of sunlight still
showed, hazing up into the deepening indigo of night. The
air which sighed in through the half-open window bore a
cold touch and there was the smell of pine on its breath.

He made his way slowly down the stairs, attracted by the fragrant smell of coffee from the dining room, went inside, found that the main table was filled and sat at one of the smaller ones against the wall.

The waitress, a girl in her late teens, brought him his food and he ate it ravenously. It was good and well-cooked and it acted as a stimulant to him. When he had finished the meal he sat back and built a smoke. The dining-room was emptying slowly and there were only a few customers still there now. He was savouring the smoke when he heard the footsteps at his back, glanced round to see Doc Horgan bearing down on him. The other took the chair across from Brad and watched soberly while the other drew deeply on the cigarette.

Then he said thoughtfully: 'I figured I might find you here. How long do you intend to stay in Medicine Reach?'

'Depends on how long it takes me to find a certain man,' said Brad, choosing his words carefully.

'You sure that he's hereabouts?'

Brad eyed the other levelly. 'I'm fairly sure. Could be that if I get the answers to some questions, I'd know for certain.'

'I don't like to see a man ride with vengeance in his heart. It only needs a little push to send him over on to the wrong side of the trail and then he has to keep running and riding, to stay one jump ahead of the law. I've seen it happen too often. I know what I'm talking about.'

'You don't understand,' Brad said slowly. He drained the last of the coffee. 'There are some things that happened a long time ago that can only be forgotten and wiped out in one way.'

'You're right,' said Horgan at last. 'I don't understand. We've got some good people here in Medicine Reach. You may not think so at the moment but they aren't sure of you. They've seen too much trouble flare up over the past few years between the nesters and the cattlemen. One side blames the other and I daresay there's something in what each side says. The cattlemen don't want the range blocked off by barbed wire, cut up into little squares, trails stopped by fences. They claim that the Government has no right to give this land to the settlers, that it's theirs by right. You'll never make them see any different.'

Brad smiled thinly. 'Like I said before, I'm not on either side. Unless the man I'm looking for happens to be. Somehow, I think he is; and I think he knows I'm here in town, looking for him.'

Horgan looked up sharply at that remark. He said tightly: 'What makes you think that?'

'The way everybody is acting. Discussing me behind my back. All talk stops as soon as I appear. A couple of riders are sent hotfoot out of town, most likely men who've been watching my every move.'

'You sure of that?'

'I'm sure.' Brad was silent for a thoughtful moment.

'This man, Frye, who owns the Lady J spread. What sort of a man is he?'

'Brett Frye? He's a reasonable man. I've heard that he tried to parley with the nesters when they first showed up around Medicine Reach, but they wouldn't talk with him and then the trouble started. He's an old man now, but I guess he still rules that place with a rod of iron. Son was in the Army during the war, made quite a name for himself, rose to be a Major under a Colonel Weekes.'

Brad felt the tightness grow within him, tried to stop it from showing on his features. 'Where's the son now? Any idea?'

'Sure. Runs the ranch most of the time. Guess it'll be his when the old man dies. Janet's his sister.' He paused, then went on. 'Sometimes, you know, I get the impression that Janet could run that spread better than her brother, Harve.'

'Why do you say that?' Brad eyed the other closely.

Horgan shrugged. 'It's difficult to put it into words. I knew him in the old days when he wasn't very old. He's younger than Janet by almost a couple of years. He was a good boy in those days, but he went off to the wars and somehow, it seems to have changed him. He's wilder now, yet there's something else too that I can't quite understand about him.'

'Like he's got something on his mind?' Brad asked.

Horgan started to shrug, then stopped and stared at him curiously, 'Why should you say that?' he murmured musingly, speaking almost as if to himself. 'That's exactly how I'd describe it. You didn't know him in the Army did you?'

'If he's the same man, then we met on one or two occasions.' Brad agreed casually.

'He can be a hard man if you cross him,' warned the other soberly. 'He sometimes rides into town with his crew. You may see him then.'

'I'll keep an eye open for him.' Scraping back his chair, he got to his feet. 'Reckon I'll go out for a breath of air before turning in,' he said.

Outside, it was not fully dark. The stars were clearly visible against the sable blackness of the heavens and there was a faintly yellow glow in the east where the moon was coming up a little past full. He walked slowly along the whole length of the street, paused at the very end, looking about him. The trail ran straight on, into low timber and then up to the hills. In the faint glow of moonlight, it gleamed whitely against the darker background. Keening around him the air that came sighing off the hills was cold and he shivered a little, pulling up the high collar of his jacket around his neck.

So it was now beginning to look as if his hunch was paying off. There was little doubt in his mind that Harvey Frye, whose father owned the Lazy J, and whose sister Janet had tended him when he was injured, was the man he had ridden almost a thousand miles to find. For some strange reason he inwardly dreaded what he would have to do. Then he remembered Lieut. Denson, Sergeant Jerrard, and those other men who had died because they had been led into a trap and he stiffened his resolution, knew that nothing was going to stop him now from getting at the truth, from killing Harvey Frye if he was the man.

How long he stood there in the cold, sweeping wind, he did not know. The moon lifted clear of the undulating horizon, flooding everything with a pale, eerie light, picking out the winding trail even more clearly. He was on the point of turning and heading back to the hotel, when he heard the distant murmur of oncoming riders. A few moments later, in the moonlight, he was able to make out the faint cloud of dust which lifted at the point where the trail emerged from the low timber in the foothills.

Stepping off the street and into the moon-thrown shadow of a deserted store, he stood against the sloping wooden wall. feeling a trace of restlessness riding him as he pressed himself against the wood. The riders, a dark scatter of them, came riding into town, passing within a few feet of where he stood. They rode by swiftly, heads lowered, hats pulled well down so that the wide brims sheltered their faces from watching eyes. Behind them, the harsh, arid dust hung in the air, stung the back of his nostrils and throat. He heard one man's harsh voice yell something unintelligible as they swung past and in the faint light, caught a glimpse of the last man in the bunch as the other lifted his head momentarily to stare directly ahead of him.

There was no mistaking the other. It was the short, squat man who had held him up at gunpoint in the canyon and then helped to beat him up, thoroughly and systematically.

They rode on down the street, then made a sudden milling stop in front of the saloon, dismounting and pushing their way through the doors. One man, Brad noticed, moved away from the others and went across to the Sheriff's office, opened the door without knocking and stepped inside. The yellow light fell on his face for a second, but he was too far away for Brad to recognize him.

For a long five minutes Brad stayed where he was. Then he walked back along the boardwalk, listening to the murmur of men's voices from the direction of the saloon, the tinkling of a piano and a woman's voice, suddenly lifting from the other sounds, clear and sweet. He left the noises behind, went up to the hotel, took his key from the clerk, said conversationally: 'Quite a bunch just rode into town. Seems like they have something to celebrate.'

'They often come here,' said the other disinterestedly. 'It'll be Harvey Frye and some of his boys. I guess.'

'Are they likely to cause any trouble?'

The other pondered that for a moment, then shook his head. 'Could wake you up around midnight with a little gunfire, but I reckon that's their limit.'

Nodding, Brad made his way up to his room. Inwardly, there was a little imp of suspicion ticking at him, giving him little rest. That man who had gone over to have a word with Sheriff Hansett? Had it been Harvey Frye? If so, what did he want with the law – and was this visit of Frye and some of his men in any way connected with those two riders who had earlier that evening ridden out of town with so much haste?

They were questions he could not answer, and he decided to get some sleep and leave them until the morning. Pulling off his boots, he sat on the edge of the bed and removed his jacket and shirt, then his pants, stretching himself out luxuriously under the sheets. They lay cool and soothing next to his body. Outside, there was the sound of a buckboard going by in the street. From across the road came the sound of singing. Evidently the men from the Lazy J were determined to enjoy themselves to the full when they were in town.

He lay for a long period, turning things over in his mind. There were some things he did not want to think about; such as Janet Frye being the sister of a man like Harvey Frye, a possible traitor to the Confederate cause. Naturally there were some who would maintain that the war was over, that the differences should be buried and forgotten, all old emnities laid aside while men of both North and South strove to work together and build something better out of what remained. But for him, this was a personal thing, something which could not be forgotten or pushed on one side, and treated as if it had never happened. It was engrained too deeply in his mind, had formed a scar there which could never heal until the man who had perpetrated this great wrong had received his due reward. But if he was right, it was going to hurt Janet Frye and possibly her father. He doubted if Harvey would have told either of them of this incident, it was not the sort of thing a man would brag about.

He rolled over on to his side, aware that the noise from the saloon across the street had faded to a low murmur with only an occasional shout sounding now and again. But sleep failed to come even though there was a deep-seated weariness in his bones. He stirred restlessly under the blankets, told himself firmly that whatever the problems they would have to wait until the morrow.

At last he fell into a dreamless doze, from which he was rudely wakened some unguessable time later by a gust of frigid air that swept across the room, touching him with its chill. He opened his eyes, saw that it was still dark with just a faint glow of moonlight filtering into the room. For a moment he lay there, shivering a little, trying to gauge where the wind had come from. Then he saw that the windows had swung open, the thin curtains blowing into the room. Puzzled, he swung his legs to the floor, moved across the room. He was halfway there when the awareness that something was wrong came to him. It was as though he had suddenly walked into a circle of wolves laying in ambush for him. A shadowy figure rose up from the balcony outside the open windows and others, three inside the room, the others outside on the balcony, closed in on him from all sides, menacing, fast and vicious.

A boot swung, caught him on the chin, knocking him off balance. He staggered, hit the side of the bed with his arm, dropped on to his back on the blankets as one of the men leapt at him, arm upraised. The butt of the pistol caught him a glancing blow on the side of the face as he jerked his head instinctively to one side. It was a truly wicked blow, designed to knock him out. Instead, it merely filled the side of his face with fire and pain, but had the redeeming features of shocking the stunned surprise from his mind. Now his brain was working fast and cold. Drawing up his legs, he planted his feet squarely in the attacker's stomach, kicked out with all of his strength. The man yelled thinly, spun through the air, knocking aside several of the others before he ended up against the wall, where he hung for a moment, then slid down on to his knees.

The brief respite gave Brad a chance to take in the position of the others in the room. There was one man near the windows who seemed to be taking no part in the attack as yet. His face was in shadow and he seemed to be watching the street down below. Evidently these men did not want to be interrupted in their vicious assault and he was keeping a sharp look out for trouble.

There were four other men around Brad now, tangled together by the fifth, who lay slumped against the wall where Brad's thrust had propelled him. One of the group swung his bunched fists at Brad's head, but he was blocked off from doing any really effective damage by the press of other bodies struggling to get to their feet and join in the slashing attack. Sucking in a deep breath, Brad fumbled for the guns which Doc Horgan had given him. His fingers closed around the butt of one of them but it was kicked from his grasp by one of the men, sent spinning into a corner of the room.

Another kick on the hip sent a stab of pain lancing through his right leg. Stung by the agony, he kicked out savagely. One of the men staggered back, uttering a shrill bleat of agony, clutching at his groin, bent double at the waist. Now there was a blind urge to destroy filling Brad's thoughts, obliterating everything else. He swung himself up off the bed with a gigantic, superhuman heave. clawed forward with one outstretched hand, found a throat and hung on desperately, squeezing inexorably. The man coughed and choked, tried to pull his fingers apart, prising at his thumbs. Brad gritted his teeth, used his other hand as a tightly clenched club, swinging and smashing at the press of faces around him. For a moment they gave under the vicious, brutal resistance, then the man at the window growled harshly: 'Finish the job – and hurry! We don't have all night to waste.'

Brad stiffened, his vague suspicions suddenly confirmed, crystallizing in his mind. That had been the voice of the short, squat man who had beaten him up on the trail. He swung away from the group facing him, lunged for the other with a blind, reckless fury. It was a mistake on his part. He knew it almost as soon as he reached the window. There was a sudden shout at his back and even as he caught hold of the man in front of him, somebody crashed him from behind, clubbing him savagely across the base of the skull. The darkness was filled with soaring stars as he dropped to his knees. Now it was a doomed and losing fight. He could not hope to hold off all of these men. The man who had fallen against the wall had got groggily to his feet and was moving forward again, his eyes filled with a murderous hate. The cumulative effect of the savage blows he had received, was beginning to tell on him now. Even though his flesh had taken on that surface numbness so that he scarcely felt any of the other blows, he was clumsy and slow in his actions. His swinging fists missed more often than they connected. No longer was he able to pick out the vague shadowy forms in front of him. There was simply and overall greyness, shot through with flashing lights and pain. Soon it would be the finish for him.

A voice said tightly: 'We warned you before, mister. Seems you don't take a tellin' easy.'

One of the men leaned over him, aimed a kick at his back. With a conscious effort, he rolled to one side, collided with another man's feet. A fist hammered off his chest, but he had avoided the crippling blow aimed at his kidneys. There came a muttered curse, the boot was drawn back again for another blow, one which could not miss this time, as he was held firmly against the other man's legs. But before the man could deliver the kick, there was a sudden and unexpected interruption.

The door of the room swung open with a crash of splintering wood. Moments later a harsh, warning voice shouted: 'Stand away from him – all of you!'

Dimly, Brad was aware of the men moving back, tautly alert, facing this new menace. With an effort, he pulled himself up on to his knees, stared towards the door. The gaunt figure standing there was immediately recognizable, even through pain-blurred eyes. Doc Horgan, the weapon in his hands levelled at the men who stood blinking in the yellow light that shafted into the room from the corridor outside.

'Keep out of this, Doc,' said the man near the window. 'We warned this *hombre* before, but he didn't heed the warning. Now we figure we've got to make it stick. Best go back to bed and forget this.' There was a note of menace in the other's voice.

Brad stayed where he was. He knew that all of these men were armed, that if thwarted, they would not stop at shooting the old doctor. What chance did a man with a rifle have against them? Then he blinked the sweat from his eyes, looked again and saw why none of the men would attempt to go against the other.

It was no rifle that Doc Horgan held tightly in his hands, but a sawed-off Greener gun, the twin barrels covering the men, a deadly weapon which could send two devastating blasts of buckshot into these men. Once, in the past, he had seen a man who had been killed by a single blast from one of these guns, usually carried by the men who rode the stage expresses. The crumpled, buckshot-riddled figure had only remotely resembled a man, flesh torn and lacerated to a frightful degree. He could understand why none of these men made any attempt to get his hand near one of his guns.

'I don't intend to tell you again,' said Horgan tightly. 'These odds are a little too biased for my liking. Now either get out the way you came in, or by God I swear I'll let you have both barrels of buckshot. Now get!'

The man at the window said in a tone of thwarted anger: 'You'll regret this, Horgan. Come tomorrow and you'll wish that you were dead.'

'If I squeeze these triggers, you will be as sure as hell,' grated the other. He moved the gun menacingly, watched through impassive eyes as the man edged back to the window.

One of them said hoarsely: 'I guess we did what we set out to do. Let's go. Nothin' more to do here. I reckon he's learned his lesson this time.'

Clearly these men did not care to gamble with this new threat that faced them and one by one they climbed out on to the balcony, let themselves down to the street. Weakly, Brad pulled himself to his feet as the Doctor went over to the window, peering down into the moonlight.

Vaguely, he picked out the muttering departure of hoofbeats in the night as the men rode out of town, heading north.

'Better try to stand up,' said Horgan, turning. He placed a hand under Brad's arm and urged him to his feet, holding him there with an effort as the other swayed and would have fallen but for his grip.

'You know who they were, Doc?' Brad asked through swollen lips. 'Did you recognize any of them?'

'Sure. It was some of the Lazy J bunch. Why'd they want to do this? You had a run in with them before?'

'With two of them,' Brad said thickly, rubbing the back of his hand over his mouth. 'Seems they've got some kind of grudge against me. Reckon I know what it could be, too.'

Horgan lifted his brows in mute interrogation. Then he said: 'They're a bad lot to tangle with, most of them rene-gades of some breed. Wouldn't be surprised if they aren't wanted in half a dozen states on some charge or other.' The thought must have sparked off a train of ideas in his mind for he went on in a sharper tone. 'You're not a lawman, are you?'

'No, I'm not toting a star.' Brad shook his head, winc-ing a little as pain jarred through it. He edged across to the thick china wash basin and the pitcher of water, half filled the basin and splashed his face and neck with the ice-cold water. His face stung at first, then things were a little better.

He dried himself on the rough towel, then went across to the window, peering out. The street lay in darkness except where the moonlight slanted down between the shadowed buildings. The men who had lain in wait and attacked him were gone, now riding out through the dark-ness to the Lazy J ranch.

'Feel like talking any?' asked Horgan. 'Maybe sleep would be the best for you, but I judge that you won't find it easy going. Talking might help you though. I'm usually a good listener. Got to be in my profession.'

'There's not much to tell,' Brad said, convinced now

that this was a man he could trust. 'Down south in Texas my name is well known. It's not an honourable name now.'

'Something to do with the war?' asked the other quietly. He seated himself in the chair, leaned forward, interested.

Brad nodded. 'I was in command of a gold shipment which had to be taken through the Yankee lines. It was essential that it should get through and only three men knew of the nature of the sealed orders I carried, orders which were not to be opened until we were a day out on the trail. Briefly, somebody gave the information to the enemy and they were waiting for us. Every man with that wagon train was killed except me. They overlooked me in the brush and when there was nothing more for me to do, when it was completely and utterly hopeless, I slipped away. I wanted only one thing then, to get back to Headquarters and warn them there was a traitor there, passing this information to the enemy.

'Colonel Weekes, my commanding officer, charged me with treason. He claimed that apart from himself and me, there was only his aide who knew of the nature of the sealed orders. He trusted his aide completely and the fact that I was the only survivor of the attack, that I was unharmed, supported his conviction that I had given the information to the Yankees. The verdict was death, a sentence which was commuted when Headquarters found there was insufficient evidence against me. But since that day, the brand of coward has stuck with me. All these years I've been looking for that other man. Either he is the traitor, or he knows who is – and I mean to find out which before I leave here.'

Horgan stared at him for a long moment in the faint light, his face taut and strained. Then he muttered: 'That man is Harvey Frye, isn't it?'

'Yes.'

Horgan got heavily to his feet. 'I knew there had to be something like this,' he said eventually. 'He had changed a lot when he came back from the war. He wouldn't talk about it, but you could see he had something on his mind, something he could never forget.'

'And this ranch, one of the biggest in these parts,' prompted Brad. 'Seems to me his father must be extremely wealthy.'

'Not exactly. It was only a small place before the war and for a little while afterwards. Not until Harvey came home did they start to build up their stock. Now they must have more than four thousand head.'

'Some achievement,' Brad commented. 'No doubt Harvey had plenty of money when he came out of the Army, though that seems a little strange, considering how impoverished the Southern states are now that the war has gone against them.'

'Now you come to mention it, it does seem curious that he could have got all of that money,' mused the other. He got to his feet and took a quick turn around the room. 'You reckon this backs up your idea that he turned over all of this important information to the North and received good money for it.'

'Seems a logical conclusion to draw,' said Brad dryly. 'It's something I mean to find out pretty soon.'

'How?'

Brad chose his reply carefully. 'The only place I can get any answers to my questions is obviously at the Lazy J. I'll ride out there tomorrow.'

'Don't you think that'll be askin' for trouble?' queried the other. 'Those riders nearly finished you tonight. Once you're out there on their home ground, they'd have no trouble.'

'Could be,' he admitted. 'But when you're hunting a mountain cat, the best place to get him is in his own lair, where you know just where he is. I came into town looking only for one man, trying to find the answers to some of my questions. This was between him and me, there was no need for anybody else to be dragged into it; but it seems I'm up against not only Frye, but the town and every man on his payroll. Those are odds I don't like. From now on, I'm going to play things their way.'

'Be careful that you don't bite off a lot more than you can chew,' warned the other. 'I can understand why you've got this thirst for vengeance against Frye. Guess I'd feel exactly the same way if it had happened to me. But they can make mighty big trouble.'

'I'll be careful.' Brad watched as the other picked up the Greener from where it was propped against the wall near the windows and made his way towards the lock-splintered door. 'Thanks for what you did tonight. I guess if you hadn't come along when you did, I wouldn't be here now.'

'Just so long as you don't do anything foolish as far as the Lazy J hands are concerned,' warned the other. He gave a brief nod, stepped out into the corridor. A moment later Brad heard his footfalls fade into the distance; then there was the faint creak of the stairs.

The next morning, shortly after the sun was up, he made his way along the street to the livery stables, picked up his mount, threw the saddle over the bay and rode out of town, heading north towards the hill trail. Slowly, the dust settled behind him. The groom watched him go with curious eyes, was on the point of turning back into the cool dimness of the stable when he spotted the Sheriff hurrying from his office towards him.

'Howdy, Sheriff,' he greeted. 'You seem in a mighty hurry.'

'That *hombre* who just rode out on the bay. Was it Calder?'

'Sure was,' agreed the other. He twisted a bite of tobacco from the black wad and began to chew it slowly. 'Like you, he seemed in a goddamned hurry.'

'Did he happen to say where he was headed?'

demanded the other, letting his gaze roam along the quiet street.

'Nope.' The other shook his head, squinted up at the sun. 'Though if you was to ask me, he's headed for the Lazy J – and he's lookin' for trouble. Seems all-fired up about somethin'. Can't say I blame him after what happened in the night.'

Hansett drew his thick brows together into a straight line. 'What about last night?' he asked thinly.

The groom smiled craftily. 'Thought you'd have heard all about it. Sheriff. There was some kind of ruckus in the hotel. A bunch of the Lazy J riders got in through the window of Calder's room. They must've climbed up on to the balcony. Started to beat him up again, might've finished him this time, only Doc Horgan busted in on them with a Greener, threatened to blow half of 'em to Kingdom Come if they didn't get out pronto.' His smile widened. 'Knowin' those coyotes, I'd say they went without any more trouble.'

Hansett's face assumed a serious expression. 'So that's the way of it,' he murmured softly, half to himself. He rubbed a hand across his face. 'Maybe I'd better get out there and try to stop any bloodshed. In his present state there's no tellin' what he might try to do.'

He waited until the other had brought his mount out of the stables, then swung up into the saddle and rode out of Medicine Reach, following Brad's trail.

Leaving town, Brad took a cut-off which angled deeper and deeper into the looming hills. Here he let the bay have its own pace, climbing through a wide funnel of timber, the branches meeting overhead in a thick, almost impenetrable carpet of twigs and leaves, through which the sunlight seldom succeeded in penetrating. Even now, with the sun lifting higher into the heavens, some of the night coolness still lay among the trees and the damp smells of the tangled vegetation touched at his nostrils, lingering with him all the way through the timber.

All about him, as the sun continued its climbing, the world was warming in the growing heat. He felt some of the heat touch him as he rode across a wide clearing, sunlight beating down at him, laying a fan of light and warmth over him. Then the timber swallowed him up once more and he knew that he was nearing the crest of the hill, that soon the trail would begin its downgrade dip. He sat loose and easy in the saddle. Once he thought he heard the sound of a rider behind him and had even paused to listen, but the sound was not repeated and a deep stillness lay all about him as if everything was still asleep, not yet wakened to the new day which had burst upon them.

In the dust of the trail he saw plenty of signs. Several men had ridden this way not too many hours before, had ridden fast and hard, pushing their horses to the limit. He did not doubt that it had been the crew from the Lazy J. Had they been headed back to the ranch perhaps, to report to Harvey Frye that their mission had failed once more, that they had been baulked in their attempt to finish him by Doc Horgan and his Greener? If so, what would Frye be planning for him this time?

Questions, but still no sound answers. He turned the thought over in his mind, then smiled grimly to himself. Certainly, the other would not be expecting him to come riding right up to the ranch like this and maybe it could throw the other sufficiently off balance to give Brad the initiative. He did not think that Frye would dare to do anything so long as he was on the Lazy J ranch. If he tried, either his father or sister would know and that was something he would want to keep from them for as long as possible. Any trouble, and he would have some awkward questions to answer from his family.

Over the brow of a hill he found himself looking down

on to a wide valley that stretched away as far as the eye could see. It was not flat, but full of undulating curves, filled with the rich green grass on which herds of cattle grazed peacefully in the flooding sunlight. He saw the men riding the rim of the herds, many of them too distant to be anything more than irregular black masses on the sides of the hills. Searching, he spotted the ranch house, a hazy smudge in the distance, shimmering in the heat haze that lay over everything. The trail wound its way over the low hills, all the way up to the ranch house, and beyond.

He rested up for a moment, then made himself a smoke and thrust it between his lips, lighting it and drawing deeply on the cigarette. Gently he touched a bruise on his jaw, worked it for a moment.

Well, he reflected tautly; he might as well get it over with. There were none of the hired hands anywhere near the road, so it looked as though he had a good chance of making it to the house without being stopped. Once there he would have to play his hand carefully. At the moment he was not even sure of what cards he held.

Gigging the bay, he rode down the slope of the hill, past a clump of irregular bushes which grew close up against it, feeling the sunlight warm and soothing on his back. As the distance decreased he saw that the ranch was a larger place than he had imagined. Even the house itself seemed to have been recently added to, enlarged by the addition of another section, joined neatly on to what was evidently the old building. It was, he noticed with a feeling of bitterness, built in the southern style. Maybe that gave Harvey Frye something with which to assuage his conscience.

There was a large corral in front of the long building, a dirt courtyard between it and the house and two barns fronting on to the bunkhouse. Several horses were in the corral and there was a buckboard standing in front of the porch, with a couple of horses in the traces. Either someone had recently arrived or was on the point of leaving for

town. He had been riding at a slow trot. Now he put his
mount to a run, as though afraid that even now, so close to
the place, one of the hired hands might pop up and try to
stop him getting there. Inwardly he felt a little surprised
that he had managed to get this far without being seen. If
the Lazy J men were afraid of being jumped by the nesters,
surely they would have posted look-outs to keep a watch
along the trails.

Reining up in front of the porch, close beside the buckboard, he sat tall and still in the saddle, knowing that his
arrival there had been noticed. A few moments later the
door opened and a man came out on to the porch. Tall
and thin, holding himself stiffly erect, he moved with an
odd deliberateness, the sunlight gleaming on his
snowwhite hair. His moustache drooped a little, giving
him a curiously sad expression, but his eyes were still
vitally alive, a piercing grey as they swept over the rider
facing him.

Brad opened his mouth to speak, but at that moment
there was another movement in the open doorway and
Janet Frye stepped out on to the porch beside her father.
She watched Brad closely with a puzzled expression on her
face and for a moment he thought he detected a look of
fear there too. Then said quietly:

'Mister Calder. Why are you here?'

Brad gave a thin smile. He said calmly: 'I thought that,
as some of the men hired by your father seem anxious to
kill me, I'd better ride out here and find out for myself
what it's all about.'

The girl looked quickly at her father as the old man
said: 'I'm afraid I don't understard. Why should any of my
men try to kill you? Who are you, sir, and what do you want
here?'

'My name is Calder. Brad Calder. You may not know me,
sir. But I assure you that your son does. Is he here? If so,
I'd like to speak to him.'

'You were with him in the war?' It was more of a state-ment than a question, but Brad nodded.

'We fought together for a time. I was in the Conederate Army too.'

'I see. But the war has been over for a long time now and everyone is trying to forget what happened. However, if you're looking for a job, I can offer you one. You no doubt know that we've been having trouble with the nesters, that they've killed several of my men and run off almost two hundred head of cattle.' His gaze became suddenly shrewd as Brad sat there, stone-still, saying noth-ing.

At last, the old man said tightly: 'That isn't why you're here, is it, Mister Calder? You've got some other kind of business with my son.'

'Yes.' Brad saw the girl's face tighten just a shade at that single word. He noticed the way her hands clenched tightly by her sides.

'Then perhaps you'd better step down and come inside.' The other moved down into the courtyard, signalled to Brad to alight.

Even as Brad eased a leg across the saddle, a familiar voice from the far side of the courtyard snapped: 'Just stay right up there, Calder. I can guess why you're here. I heard you were snooping around town, asking questions, even after you'd been warned off once.'

Brad turned, faced the other. Harvey Frye had stepped out of the shadows between the two barns. There was a Winchester in his hands, the barrel pointed straight at Brad's chest. His lips were thinned back in a vicious snarl.

'Put up that gun,' snapped Brett Frye. 'There'll be no shooting here on this ranch. I asked this man inside and I mean to get to the bottom of this – who he is and why he's come here.'

'I want him off this spread right now,' said the other stubbornly. The rifle in his hands did not budge. 'And my say-so is enough. Don't forget that the money for the spread is mine. You had nothing. I'm the real boss here, not you, Father.'

'And where did that money come from?' asked Brad pointedly. 'Could it have been pay you received from the Yankees for services rendered during the war?'

'Shut up!' The other's face suddenly drained of colour. There was a bright glint in his eyes and the finger on the trigger tightened, knuckle standing out with the pressure he was exerting. 'I won't tell you again, Calder. If you want to stay alive, turn that horse of yours around and ride out of here – pronto. Keep riding once you get off this spread. If I hear that you've stopped in Medicine Reach again, there'll be a third time and then you won't be so lucky.'

Brad shook his head slowly, his gaze beating the other down. 'You don't dare kill me here, Harvey,' he said thinly. 'This time there are too many witnesses. So you shoot me down in cold blood. What do you do then? Shoot your father and sister too? They might talk and more than that, they might want to know who Brad Calder really is and why he came here, all the way from Texas, just looking for you.'

'Damn you, Calder!' The other took a couple of paces forward, lifting the rifle slightly in his hands. 'I won't tell you again.'

'You'll put that rifle down and listen to reason.' Brad switched his glance towards the old man. Unseen by either of them, the other had drawn his heavy, long-barrelled Colt. It was aimed directly at his son's heart. 'I don't know who this man is, but I intend to hear what he has to say. It looks to me as if he's been beaten up and I know that Telfer and some of the boys rode back here during the early hours of the morning. If there was trouble in town, I want to know what it was about.'

'You going to listen to a man like that?' snapped Harvey Frye thinly. Reluctantly, seeing the look on his father's face, he lowered the rifle to his side. 'You've heard of Brad Calder, the man who sold our secrets to the Yankees, the man who led the last gold shipment out into their hands. Nine men were killed then. They never had a chance. Yet he got free with a whole skin, even came back into camp riding one of their horses, claimed he'd managed to escape, wanted to warn us about a traitor at Headquarters who thought we didn't have quite enough evidence against him that the charge was reduced to one of cowardice in the face of the enemy. Is that the kind of man you're going to believe?'

For a moment Brett Frye stood silent, his gaze switching from his son's face to Brad's. Then he said slowly, through tightly clenched teeth. 'Are you that man, the one found guilty of cowardice?'

'I'm Brad Calder,' he said simply. 'I'm the man they accused of cowardice. I'm here in an attempt to clear my name. I reckon every man has a right to do that if he's in the same position as I am.'

Brett Frye pursed his lips, considered that for a moment, then jerked a thumb towards the door. 'Get down, mister; and step inside.' He threw a quick glance at his son. 'I intend to hear what he's got to say, Harve. I'll know if he's telling the truth. If he's lying, then I reckon you might just be right about running him out of the territory. If there's anything I hate worse'n a rattler, it's a coward.'

'You're being a goddamned fool,' said Harvey Frye. He glared across at Brad. His eyes were sultry coals behind the hooded lids and there was very little expression on his features. Something had happened to this man since Brad had last seen him, something he had not expected to see. The other had let go of something which had once held him to a reasonable respect and responsibility. Now he was a man continually on the defensive, a man shadowed and haunted by his past, and a little fearful of his future.

Swinging to the courtyard, he tethered his mount to the hitching rail and stepped up on to the porch. All the time he was acutely aware of the sultry figure of Harvey Frye standing a few yards away, watching his every move, still holding on to the rifle as if he intended to use it at any moment.

The old man followed him inside, pointed to a room leading off the wide corridor. Once inside, he closed the door, motioned to a chair and sat down himself, easing a stiff right leg out in front of him.

'Very well, Mister Calder,' he said harshly. 'I'll hear what you have to say. From what happened out there, I gather that it has something to do with my son. I'd be glad if you'd speak your piece as quickly as possible.'

'Of course, sir.' Brad nodded. There was something about this man which seemed solid and dependable. Not quite like his son, although there was the same cut of the features there. He held his hat in his hands, staring down at it as he began: 'I served in the same regiment as your son during the war. It was shortly after the Battle of the Wilderness. I was ordered to take a gold shipment through the enemy lines, using a route which lay well off the main trails and which offered a good chance of success. My orders were in a sealed package and it was to be opened only after we had been a day's march on the trail. Only three people knew the contents of that package before we set out. Colonel Weekes, myself and your son.' He hesitated, eased himself back in his chair, watching the other's face for a long moment.

Finally, Brett Frye stirred, said thinly: 'Go on. What happened?'

'We were betrayed. There's no doubt in my mind about that, the Yankees were waiting for us along the trail, it was impossible to hold them off. There were too many of them and the trap had been well laid. I knew that somehow, word would have to be got back to the regiment. When I saw that nothing could be done for any of the others, I knocked out one of their sentries, stole a horse and made my way back to the camp.'

'And you were accused of treason as soon as you rode in?'

'Yes. Colonel Weekes had absolute faith in your son. I was the only other person to know what had been in that sealed package and since I was the only one to survive that attack, everything was against me. As your son says, had it not been for lack of evidence, I would have been shot out of hand.'

'Yet you have no proof that you did not give that information to the enemy,' murmured the other, his gaze questing, probing Brad's face.

'I don't expect you to believe me against the word of your son. When I came here, my only intention was to face your son and demand the answers to my questions. I want to clear my name and see that the real traitor is punished in the only proper way.'

'You want to act as jury, judge and executioner? Even though the war has been over for some years now and the country, both sides are striving to live in peace and harmony and trying to rebuild a better country.'

'I can't forget that I've been branded a coward. I've been disowned by my family, shunned by ordinary people who know me by name and reputation. Do you think a man can go on living like that for the rest of his life, without trying to do something to clear himself?'

'You put me in a very difficult position,' said the other. He sighed and got stiffly to his feet, walked over to the window looking out into the sunlit courtyard. 'You can't expect me to hand over my son to you, just on your say-so. He obviously isn't going to admit to this charge you've levelled against him, even if it happens to be true.'

'Happens to be true.' Brad smiled thinly. 'Since I rode into this territory I've been brutally attacked twice. Once

when I was on the trail into Medicine Reach and once in
the hotel there – last night. On both occasions it was men
from the Lazy J who did their best to beat me to death. If
your son didn't ask them to do it, then who did? I don't
know any of the other men on your payroll, yet they
seemed determined to kill me.'

Brett Frye turned, looked at him levelly in the sunlight
that came streaming in through the window. It was obvious
from the bruises that showed on Brad's face that this part
of his story was true. He sighed audibly. 'Come with me,'
he said eventually.

Going out into the courtyard, he stood in front of the
porch, a tall, weather-beaten man, still with pride in his
bearing.

'Harvey!' he called loudly.

There was a moment's silence. Then the other stepped
into view from the bunkhouse. He had left his rifle
behind, but there were two guns strapped to his waist and
his face had lost none of its earlier surly look.

'Well?' he demanded. 'Have you heard his lies?'

'I've listened to his version of what happened,' said the
older man slowly. 'I don't think he's lying. But perhaps you
can explain why these attempts have been made to beat
him up. Just to frighten him off? If that's so, why scare him
away unless he knows something you're afraid of.'

'You know nothing about this, father,' said the other
tautly. 'I knew what would happen the minute Calder rode
in here. I knew he was riding up from Texas, that he'd
come looking for me sooner or later, and I knew that when
he did he would have a gun in his fist and it would be
aimed at me. It doesn't matter much what I say now, he'll
never believe that it wasn't me who betrayed that secret
route which the shipment was taking.'

'So you deliberately tried to frighten me off.' Brad shook
his head. 'I don't believe that for one minute. You'd never
go to those lengths if there was no truth in what I believe.'

'Why not?' burst out the other vehemently. 'You were branded a coward by the regimental officers. I had no hand in that. I was not even called as a witness. Colonel Weekes put the position to them and he was determined that you should be shot. You don't know how angry he was when the word came down the line that you were to be tried on a lesser charge, that they didn't consider there was enough evidence to convict you of treason.'

'Then if you weren't the traitor, who was?' flared Brad. He had an instinctive feeling that the other was hedging, was holding something back.

'How should I know? All I can tell you is that I had nothing to do with it. I knew you blamed me for it. I have ways of knowing what goes on, even down in Texas, and I knew when you started riding north to find me. You meant to kill me then for what happened; and you mean to kill me now. Oh, you may have told my father that all you want is the truth, and he may even believe you. But I know better. That's why I'm warning you to get out of this territory and stay out if you want to remain alive.'

Brad looked him up and down. He drew his lips slightly. 'So you still make the big threat, Harvey, still try to look as if you own all of this range, and you don't like me being here because you figure I'm getting on to something you'd like best to keep hidden. Well I don't scare that easy as these boys of yours will find out if they ever try to come after me again. You and the rest want to play things rough, well that's how I intend to play them from now on. You know something about what happened and because of those nine men who died with that wagon train, I don't aim to leave until I find out what it is.'

Turning, he went over to where his mount was tethered, untied the rope from around the hitching rail, keeping his back deliberately to the other. Swinging up into the saddle, he finally turned and stared down at the two men. 'Don't forget what I've said,' he murmured softly, ominously. 'I didn't ride into Medicine Reach deliberately looking for trouble, but if it's there then I'm more than ready to meet it halfway.'

Harvey Frye sucked in a deep breath, cheeks flattening against the bones of his face. For a moment he seemed on the point of going for his guns. His hands hung close above them, fingers clawed. Then he forced himself to relax sharply as Brad said: 'If you feel like ending it here and now, go ahead. I'm ready.'

Harvey Frye shook his head slowly, not once taking his eyes from Brad's face. There was a sneer to his tone as he said: 'I reckon you've probably had a lot more experience with guns than I have. I don't aim to give you the pleasure of shooting me down in cold blood. But if you figure that you'll stick around in spite of what I've said, then I figure you've just dug your own grave.'

'We'll see.' Touching spurs to his mount, Brad rode out of the dusty courtyard, headed into the sun, back towards the distant hills on the skyline. He felt an angry bitterness as he rode; he had come out here to get at the truth, and now he was riding back, no closer to it than when he had come.

4

RENEGADE COUNTRY

The noon sun burned down on the open country that lay just beyond the timber line. Coming out of the trees, Brad reined his horse abruptly as he caught sight of the dust cloud on the trail ahead of him. He could not identify the rider from that distance, but there was the possibility that it meant trouble and he drew back from the trail, deeper into the trees, holding himself still as he waited, one of the Colts withdrawn from its holster, the hammer thumbed back.

Slowly the rider came on, the steady abrasion of his horse's hoofbeats sounding clearly in the stillness. As the other drew nearer Brad saw that his horse was lame, had probably thrown a shoe. One of the Lazy J ranch-hands, heading back from town? The thought passed through his mind as he watched the other's approach. Not until the man was almost on his hiding place did he recognize the tall, burly figure who sat astride the saddle, his face lined and masked with dust.

Gigging his mount out on to the trail, he said genially: 'Howdy, Sheriff. Looking for me?'

The other started, pulling hard on the reins, bringing his mount to a sliding halt. His hand, on the point of darting down towards his gun, halted in mid-air. With an effort he relaxed. 'Don't ever do a foolish thing like that again, Calder,' he said. 'You might get yourself shot if you do.'

'You'd have been minutes late,' Brad said harshly, 'Just why are you trailing me, Sheriff?'

'What makes you think it's you I want to see?' muttered the other. 'Could be that I have business with Frye.'

'Which one? The father or the son?'

'All right, all right. So I figured you might start somethin' out there that you couldn't finish and I didn't want any trouble.' The other pulled a handkerchief from his pocket and mopped his brow. 'The groom reckoned you were headed for the Lazy J and knowing what happened last night, I guessed you might have decided to take the law into your own hands, in spite of the warnin' I gave you.'

Brad smiled thinly. 'From what I've seen in Medicine Reach, the law is always a little late in giving protection to its citizens. Even if they're only strangers in town.'

Hansett growled something unintelligible under his breath, scowling as he stared as the other. 'Seems to me that these *hombres* have got some personal grudge against you, Calder. I don't know what it is, but for your own sake and for my peace of mind, I'd be obliged if you'd ride on as soon as possible.'

'I've still got some business to settle before I leave, Sheriff.' Brad said quietly.

'That why you rode out to the Frye place? I passed Miss Janet on the way here. She said you were talking to her Pa. What's biting you, Calder?'

'Like I said before, I'm looking for a man. I figure that his name is Harvey Frye. When I knew him he was a Captain in the Confederate Army. I've got a feeling that he was a spy in the pay of the Yankees at that time, that he got me accused of it to shield himself.'

'You got any proof of that?' inquired the other. 'Anythin' that would stand up in court?'

'You know damned well I haven't, Sheriff. If I had, do you think I'd have left the Lazy J with Harvey Frye still alive?'

'Now see here, you can't go around killin' folk just because you got some flea in your bonnet that he might've been the man who betrayed you to the enemy, during the war. That's all finished and done with.'

'So everybody seems keen to tell me,' Brad said bitterly. 'The trouble is that when you've been branded a coward, the charge sticks until you can prove otherwise. Nobody so far has let me forget that.'

Hansett nodded, but said nothing further. For a moment he stared at Brad, then he wheeled his mount. 'Guess we might as well ride back into town,' he observed. 'Ain't no point in ridin' out to the Lazy J right now. Not on a lame horse.'

They reached town by mid-afternoon, with the heat head at its highest pitch of piled-up intensity. There was little activity in the main street. Out of the corner of his eye Brad noticed the loungers on the boardwalk, some seated in their tilted-back chairs, legs crossed, their hats pulled down over their eyes, others leaning against the wooden uprights, watching all that went on about them.

At the saloon hitch rail, several saddle mounts stood slack-hipped. Beneath the overhang, talk stopped as he and the Sheriff rode past. Brad drew his brows together in deep, pondering thought. Why this suspicion concerning him? Was it simply because he was a stranger here and this town did not like strangers? Or was it because he had evidently fallen foul of the powerful Lazy J ranch? He shrugged the thought away. The trail dust lay thick in his throat and he reined up at the smaller saloon halfway along the street.

'Guess I'll wash the dust out of my mouth and get me a bite to eat, Sheriff. Unless you're still not satisfied about why I was at the Frye place?'

Hansett paused, then shook his head. 'No, I guess I've got nothin' more to say right now. But I'll probably think of somethin' before the day is out.'

Stepping down from the saddle, Brad watched as the lawman rode over to the Sheriff's office and went inside. Then he moved through the swing doors of the saloon and went into the cool dimness. There were a handful of men at the bar and a few others at the tables. A poker game was in progress on the far side of the room with a group of men clustered around the card players. Brad gave them only a cursory glance. It was not until he was at the bar, leaning his elbows on it, that he noticed anything different about these men.

Not one of them was a cattleman. He tried to figure out what was different as he held up his finger to the barkeep. The other moved forward reluctantly.

'What'll it be, mister?' he asked sharply. There was no tone of welcome in his voice.

'Whisky,' Brad said slowly.

The other paused then, as if begrudging every movement he made, he bent and drew a bottle and a glass from below the bar and set them on the counter in front of him.

Brad laid down a couple of dollars. 'Cigars too,' he said, not once lowering his glance from the man's face. The other's look was blank and unrevealing. This was something that Brad did not quite understand. In the other saloon or the hotel there had been a hint of friendliness, even though it had not been very pronounced. Here there was not only a lack of it, there seemed to be a very definite animosity towards him.

He waited until the barkeep had brought the box of cigars, selected a couple of them, thrust them into his pocket and poured himself a drink while the other picked up the coins, stared at them for a long moment as if they were counterfeit, then Brad said tersely. 'All right, bartender. What's wrong here? My money the wrong colour or something?'

'Don't see anythin' wrong with your money, mister,' said the other after a distinct pause. 'But I ain't so sure about you.' His glance travelled over Brad's dust-stained clothing. 'You look like a cowhand to me. What are you doin' in here if that's the case?'

'Suppose you tell me why I shouldn't come in here and then maybe I'll answer your question.'

'What Joe's tryin' to say, mister,' rumbled a harsh voice from behind him, 'is that we're particular who comes in here. We don't want any of the Lazy J hired hands spying on us. Got that?'

Brad turned slowly, staring into the belligerent face of the man who stood a couple of yards away, feet planted well apart, obviously hungering for a fight.

'I hear you,' he said tightly, 'but I don't understand you, friend.'

'Easy won't do it,' snarled the other harshly. 'Who sent you here? Harvey Frye or his foreman? Seems to me they don't have the guts to face us openly so they get some stranger to come in, actin' all innocent, orderin' a drink and a couple of cigars, and at the same time takin' a good look around, maybe keepin' his ears open, hopin' to pick up somethin'.'

Slowly Brad let his gaze wander around the rest of the men. The card players had stopped their game, were also eyeing him with severe eyes. Then it came to him. These men were the nesters, the deadly enemies of Frye and the other ranchers.

'I get it now,' he said evenly. He turned back to the bar, drank down the whisky and then took out one of the cigars, lit it carefully and puffed the smoke out in front of him. 'I'm afraid you've got me figured all wrong. I don't work for Frye or any of the others.'

'He was hurt bad when he rode into town a few weeks ago, Abe,' called one of the card players. 'Did hear a rumour that it was some of the Lazy J men who beat him up along the trail. Could be he's tellin' the truth.'

'So he ain't exactly on friendly terms with the Lazy J riders,' said the other surlily, still not convinced. 'That don't mean he's on our side.'

Brad shrugged. 'It's a matter of no consequence to me what you believe,' he said thinly. 'I just came in here for a drink to clear my throat of trail dust. You can make anything of that you damned well please.' He felt the anger beginning to rise in him now. Too long he had been met by veiled suspicion, sometimes open animosity, in this town. It was getting close to the time when he would take it no longer, begin to give as good as he received.

Arrogance remained in the nester's eyes and there was a look of hot intolerance fuming in him. But now these things were clearly beginning to temper under a deeper caution. He studied Brad narrowly as if recognizing that the man facing him was no ordinary drifter who could be bullied and threatened easily; that he was a man with a purpose that nothing was going to steer him from.

'All right,' he conceded finally. 'So you're not a friend of theirs. But you see for yourself that we have to be careful. They're tryin' to block us at every turn. We bought the land fair and square from the Government, but these men are trying to keep it from us. They bring out phoney deeds that lay claim to the land, reckoning that they bought it from the French. While these deeds are being looked over legally, we're havin' to fight to keep our land.'

'I guess I know how you feel,' Brad said slowly. 'But that's your fight, not mine. I have only one reason for being here, to find a man.'

'And when you find him?' asked Abe, moving up to the bar.

'Then I'll kill him and that will be the end of it.' The other nodded his head slowly. Picking up the whisky bottle, he poured himself a drink, downed it at a single gulp, grimacing a little. The action was a signal for a lowering of the tension that had been building up inside the bar.

'You know who this man is?' queried the other, regarding him closely from under lowered brows.

'Not for certain – no. I've got my suspicions. I reckon it's Harvey Frye. But I've no proof of it yet.'

'Harvey Frye.' The other let his breath whistle out thinly through his teeth in surprise. 'I reckon you'll find it hard to square up any accounts with him. He has his own private army of hired killers out there at the Lazy J ranch and you can't fight all of them, no matter how hard you try, or how fast you are with a gun.'

Brad poured himself another drink, sipped it slowly this time. The liquor was forming a warm cloud in his stomach and the smoke from the cigar eased the ache in his chest. 'If Harvey Frye is the man I'm looking for,' he said ominously, 'then I'll get him, never fear.'

Abe shrugged. He seemed to have thawed completely now. 'That's your problem, I reckon,' he acknowledged. 'Can't say any of us would be sorry to see him killed. We might have arranged things peaceable like with the old man, but not with the son. He's determined to drive us off this land and he's hired all of those killers to see to it that he succeeds. There have been too many killings, too many homesteads fired by that bunch for there to any concessions made now.'

'I can understand that,' he nodded. He finished his drink. 'Guess I'll get back to the hotel for a bite to eat.'

He nodded to the rest of the men, made his way out into the street, walked his mount over to the livery stables, then went on to the hotel. Climbing the stairs to his room, he washed, put on a fresh shirt from his saddleroll, combed his hair and felt a little more refreshed. He sat in the chair by the window until the supper gong sounded downstairs, then went into the dining-room, picked a table against the wall, where he could see the door, and waited for his meal to arrive.

When it came, he ate ravenously, enjoying the taste of the well-cooked food, washing it down with three cups of the hot, strong black coffee. Outside, it was still light, with the last rays of the sun slanting over the roofs of the buildings, laying a net of red over the street as far as he could see. Overhead, the sky was clear, cloudless still, the colours changing as he watched from red and orange, through a coppery green to a deep indigo. The sun dropped behind the hills like a penny going into a black box and already the night was beginning to intrude from the east.

Taking out the second cigar he bit off the end, smoked it slowly, savouring the taste of the tobacco, drawing the smoke into his lungs. Relaxing, he leaned back in his chair, eyeing the other customers, letting his gaze move over them. None seemed to be taking any notice of him. Perhaps the fact that he had ridden back into town with the Sheriff, had allayed some of their suspicions.

For a long fifteen minutes he sat there, smoking out his cigar. After which he went back up the creaking stairs to his room. He had not locked his door when he had gone down to the dining-room and pushing it open, he stepped into the dimness, pausing for a moment to allow his eyes to become adjusted to the darkness before moving forward to light the lamp.

Just inside the doorway he stiffened, aware that there was someone in the room. Hesitating for only a second, his right hand whipped down for the gun in its holster. It was out of leather, pointed into the room, when a clear, resonant voice said: 'I'm sorry if I startled you, Mister Calder, but I have to talk with you. It's urgent.' Pushing the door shut with the palm of his left hand he moved forward slowly, saw the figure of the girl standing near the window. Then he had found a match, scraped it until it flared and lit the lamp, placing the glass funnel carefully on top of it.

Janet Frye moved away from the window and sat down in the chair. The golden light from the lamp fell on her regular features, touching them with shadow. There was still a high pride in her. He noticed that at once, in the tilt of her head, the set of her shoulders.

'I suppose you have a reason for being here?' he said, sitting on the edge of the bed.

'I think you how what it is,' she said in a very soft tone. 'I can guess how you come to be in this town. I think I know why you went to see my brother. You think that he was the one who betrayed you to the enemy.'

'How do you know all of this?' he asked, curious.

Her smile was a mere curving of her lips. It did not touch her eyes. 'I've known for some time that he's had something on his mind, something that has been troubling him more and more, ever since he came back from the war. Less than a year ago he sent two men south, into Texas. I heard him talking to them, and he mentioned the name Brad Calder. After that, he seemed to get regular reports from these men and it didn't take much imagination to guess that he was afraid of this man, afraid that sooner or later he would find out where my brother was and come riding north for him. When he heard that you were on your way here he told some of the men to keep an eye on the trail. I didn't know that he meant to have you beaten up like that. I thought he only wanted to give you a warning to stay away. But you didn't heed it and now I'm afraid of what he might do.'

'Maybe,' said Brad, not ungently, 'you might be persuaded to get him to tell me all he knows. If he isn't the man I'm looking for then there's no reason for him to be afraid.'

She made no answer to that, but continued to look down at the floor beneath her feet.

Brad tried again. 'It could only have been your brother or Colonel Weekes. There was no one else.'

'And if he were the one, would you go through with your threat? Would you kill him in cold blood?'

Now it was Brad's turn to be silent. He knew that was something he could not answer to her. She saw the look on his face and did not press him further. The uneasy silence grew then until the girl said in a hushed tone: 'I don't want you to kill my brother. I suppose that's really why I'm here, to plead with you not to go through with this. I know how you must feel, being branded a coward unjustly. But the war has been over for a long time now. Couldn't you leave things as they are here, ride on north where you're not known, start a fresh life?'

He shook his head slowly. 'I can't do that,' he said quietly. 'There are some things a man has to do, no matter what, and this is one of them.'

Janet Frye got quickly to her feet, stood for a moment looking down at him, her hands clasped in front of her, fingers intertwined. The look on her face was almost like that he would have expected to see if he had physically struck her.

'Is that your last word?' she asked at last.

He gave a quick nod which was almost brutal. 'I'm afraid that's the way it has to be,' he said numbly.

'Then I'm sorry for you,' she said, an odd edge of sharpness to her tone. She whirled away from him, and went over to the door. 'When I nursed you back to health after you'd been brought here, I guessed then who you were. Maybe I ought to have done less for you then, let you die perhaps. It would have saved me a lot of worry and trouble.'

He wanted to say something to reassure her, but there were no words for that. This was one of the hardest moments of his life. He knew that she was still standing there in the doorway of his room, silently pleading with him. Yet he could say nothing. After a few moments she went out into the corridor, closing the door behind her. Wearily he turned away and moved to the window, aware of the faint subtle perfume which still lingered in the air.

For some little time he stood beside the window looking down into the street but not really seeing anything that went on down there, his thoughts far away, conscious of his leaping pulse. The girl had had an impact on him which he had not expected and which held him now in a long and thoughtful pause. If only it had been possible for them to have met under different circumstances, he thought ruefully; but fate had decreed otherwise.

Frowning slightly, he caught the movement down below in the street. The buckboard moved away from in front of the hotel, heading north. He caught a glimpse of the girl, seated erect on the tongue of the wagon as it passed through the shafts of yellow light from the windows along the street. Only once did she half turn and look back, up at the window, but whether she saw him or not, he did not know.

He felt restless as he went back into the room, locked the door and then, remembering the night before, locked the window too. At least her brother and his men were not going to take him by surprise again. As he sat on the edge of the bed, pulling off his boots, he began wondering once more about Harvey Frye. There were so many things plotting against him, that it scarcely seemed possible that he could have been telling the truth when he had claimed that he had not betrayed him to the enemy. Yet if it were the truth, just where did that leave things?

Brad turned the idea over in his mind. It was the first time since he had taken the trail from Texas that he had considered anyone else as a possible candidate. Now he tried to think things out along these lines. At first it just failed to make any sense.

Would Colonel Weekes have done such a thing? On the

face of it, looking back on events in those days it seemed utterly ridiculous and out of the question. Certainly Weekes had been extremely anxious to have him shot, and as soon as possible. There was just the possibility that this had been the action of a guilty man, wanting to be rid of the evidence, of anyone who could speak against him. But it was still inconceivable that a man in his position would have been a traitor.

His thoughts began to turn around on themselves and he pulled off his shirt and lay back on the bed, drawing up the blankets to his chin. Outside there was very little sound in the town. None of the usual rowdies had ridden in from the hills or the outlying ranches. He tried to go on thinking things out logically, but his mind was so weary now that it refused to do so clearly and in the end he gave it up and rolled over on to his side, closing his eyes and composing himself for sleep.

He woke early the next morning, before it was full light. The clerk behind the desk in the lobby was asleep, grunted half angrily as Brad shook him awake, then took the key from him, stringing it up on the board behind him. 'You riding out right now?' he asked. When Brad nodded, he went on: 'What about breakfast?'

'Don't bother to save any for me.' Brad moved towards the outer door. 'I'll be gone most of the day.'

'All right. It's your life, I reckon.' The other settled back down in the chair, his legs curled up under him. Brad eyed him for a moment with a faint smile on his face, then swung away, went out into the dark, quiet, deserted street, heading for the livery stables. The groom was awake, the red glow of his cigarette just visible in the darkness. He stepped forward as Brad approached, peered up at him curiously.

'Get my horse for me,' Brad said sharply. 'I'm riding out.'

There was a look of beady wisdom in the other's eyes as

he pushed his lean body away from the wooden upright but he moved off obediently, came back a few minutes later, leading the bay. He handed the reins over to Brad, watched in silence as the other bent to tighten the cinch under the animal's belly. As Brad swung up into the saddle, he asked: 'You figurin' on riding up into the hills?'

'That's my business.'

'Sure, sure.' The other nodded his head swiftly, almost as if it were bobbing up and down on the end of a spring. 'Only I'd keep my eyes open if I were you. Those hills are full of renegades, bad ones all of them. They'd shoot a man in the back and ask questions later.'

'I know the kind of men,' Brad said with conviction. 'I'll be careful.' He paused then pulled out a dollar and dropped it into the other's palm. 'And this time, if Sheriff Hansett comes along asking about me, you don't know which way I've gone. Understand?'

'I ain't seen a thing,' said the other with a thin smile. He thrust the coin into his pocket, leaned back against the upright once more. The tip of his cigarette winked on and off in the night, like a tiny fist beating against the darkness.

Running upgrade, now on the road, now in the shelter of the tall timber, he reached the break of the hills long before sunup, with the housetops of Medicine Reach now some distance behind him. Although he had made up his mind what he was going to do, he was still tricked by apprehension and every tiny, rustling movement in the brush was enough to bring his head jerking round, eyes flashing in the direction of the sound.

Riding thus, he was deep into the hills when the late stars began to pale before the coming of the dawn, breaking greyly over the brim of the world. The hills began to shoulder down now, edging a little closer to the trail. Juniper dotted the lower slopes and he moved through it at a slow trot, still alert now that he was close to the perimeter fence of the Lazy J ranch. The most southerly meadow came close to the trail at this point, he recalled; and if there was a herd bedded down there for the night there might also be men cooking themselves an early breakfast, hoping to take the bite of the night's cold out of their bones.

Treading warily, his mount moved through the undergrowth as he pushed it off the trail. Low branches struck at his head and neck, vines dangling like ropes brushed against his face. Here, the darkness was still almost absolute, the trees and branches effectively shutting out the grey light of early morning. Going down out of the trees, he encountered some of the worst footing he had ever known. At one place he was forced to dismount and lead the bay forward by the reins as rough rocks broke up into vine undergrowth and then gave way to shale and loose slate. The horse followed him patiently, a surefooted animal, moving quietly over the treacherous ground. That was the way of it for a full fifteen minutes. Then, just as the grey in the east was turning to a pale rose flush, he came upon a narrow ravine that cut down at an angle to smoother ground. He took it and came out on the meadow. The perimeter wire here was badly in need of repair, with broken strands sprung back from the heavy wooden posts. Climbing back into the saddle he eased the Colts in their holsters for a moment, checked that the chambers were all loaded, then gigged the bay forward, the grass muffling any sound.

Ten minutes later the smell of a wood fire and coffee stopped him short. He held quite still, sniffing the air, then dismounted and went forward on foot, easing his way up the lee of the low hill and crouching down, he saw the small herd some five hundred yards away. Nearer at hand but still a considerable distance away, he recognized one of them as the tall, thin-faced man who had threatened him with the rifle that first day when he had ridden into these parts. For a moment he felt the rising anger in him again, felt the twitch in his fingers as they touched the cold metal of the gun at his waist. Then he forced himself to relax. This was not why he had come here.

Turning his head slowly he studied his situation, looking about him. The low hills made a slow turn into the country in the direction of the ranch house and beyond, then sloped back to the higher ridges through which he had just ridden.

Slowly, he made his way back to his mount. Apart from a couple of men who were riding herd on the cattle in the distance, he guessed there were no others within a ten-mile radius. Out of sight of the herders, he swung up once more into the saddle and as the sun lifted clear of the eastern horizon, crossed a two-mile stretch of meadow covered in wild grass, a narrow path leading down the middle. Through scattered pine stands with a deadfall here and there, he entered a draw that was narrow and overgrown with brush. Now he was well away to one side of the main trail, circling the Lazy J spread. Inside the draw he felt the gradual rise and experienced no surprise when he eventually came out on a long, smooth ridge of ground that looked down into the northern end of the wide valley, with the ranch house and outbuildings cluster together about a mile away. The valley itself lay in deep shadow although here on the ridge he was in the warm sunlight. He dismounted, led his horse back a little way so that it could not be seen from down below, then went back and lay on his stomach, smoking a cigarette as he settled down to wait. He did not know how long he would be forced to wait, but he decided to make himself comfortable in the interim.

The sun lifted slowly. Gradually the shadows fled from the valley and sunlight moved like a great wave over it, washing the darkness away. There were no clear signs of activity down below at the ranch. He could see no sign of the buckboard and guessed that Janet Frye was possibly still in town, having spent the night there after her abortive attempt to get him to ride out and forget all about her brother.

In spite of himself he found his thoughts turning back to her more than he liked. This was no time to become serious about a good-looking woman, especially if he had to kill her brother. His original idea had been simply to ride in and face up to Harvey Frye, call him and judge from his attitude, from his actions, whether or not he was the guilty man he sought. If so, then it would have been either the other man or himself. Now things had suddenly become extremely complicated. First Janet Frye had helped to nurse him when he had been beaten to within an inch of death. There had been no call for her to do a thing like that. But she had done it without question. Her father too seemed a straight and honest man.

Lying there, with the smoke from the cigarette lacing across his eyes, he turned his considerations to Harvey Frye. At the very beginning, even after meeting the other face to face after all these years, he had felt certain that he was the man. Now, curiously, on reflection, he was not so sure. It was difficult to pick out anything definite which made him change his mind. There was no doubt that Harvey Frye was afraid, scared spitless. Yet was he afraid because of something he had done, because of what Brad might to do him; or was there some other reason for his fear? It was this possibility which was troubling Brad. He gave it more thought as he smoked the cigarette down to a stub, crushing it out in the dirt in front of him. It was just possible that if something else was making Harvey Frye afraid, so scared that he had been forced to the point of trying to kill him, then he might learn something by watching any visitors the other might have. By now, things would be rapidly coming to a head. They had tried to get rid of him twice, and failed. And men who were afraid often did foolish things.

Now he waited, leaning on his left side, looking over
the smooth, grassy slope in front of him, the sunlight
growing stronger with every minute. The rocks which
jutted out here and there through the grass were clear and
clean in the morning sunlight and he could pick out the
faint sounds of birds in the trees behind him, the soft
sound of the breeze as it soughed through the swaying
branches. The grass under him was cool and damp and he
thought, feeling some of the dew soak into his shirt, that
by the time the sun has moved across the zenith, dipping
down towards the west, some of the answers to what was
puzzling him might be known.

A couple of men came out of the bunkhouse, made
their way to the corral and cut their horses out of the small
group, throwing saddles on to their backs, tightening
cinches, thrusting long-barrelled Winchesters into the
scabbards, and then swinging easily up into the saddle,
riding out south, kicking up the dust behind them as they
galloped out of the courtyard. After that, fifteen minutes
passed before there was any further sign of movement.
Brad lay there with a patience which made stone of his
body, watching the scene through unwinking eyes.

There was a large clump of trees about half a mile to
the south of the ranch house, very close to the trail. If
anybody came from that direction, he mused, any birds
would lift from the branches and give him ample warning.

A movement on the porch, just visible beneath the
wooden overhang and he recognized the tall, grey-haired
figure of Brett Frye. The old man came slowly out into the
open, moved across the courtyard to the corral and stood
with his back to Brad, leaning his body on the wooden rail-
ings, arms folded in front of him.

Brett Frye was an enigma, Brad thought idly; a man he
had not been really able to figure properly. There was little
doubt that he tried to wield an iron hand over the Lazy J
ranch and the men employed there, but if it were true that

most of the money that had gone into the place belonged to Harvey, then it would not be easy for him. He could understand some of the sadness which he had seen on the other's lined face. Sardonic pressure thinned his lips. It was more than likely that these killers who had been brought into the Lazy J fold, had been hired by Harvey, not his father. What the other thought about it he could not imagine.

There was a sudden rising of a flock of birds from the distant trees. They lifted as one, swooped low and circled the area before slowly returning. He stared out through narrowed eyes, felt the growing tightness in his body, then relaxed a little as he saw the buckboard come out of the trees, along the trail, dust rising like smoke behind it. Janet Frye returning from town. He sank back on to the ground, rolled himself another cigarette, thrust it between his lips and held it there without lighting it. He could feel his shoulders pulled up tense and told himself to relax, thinking: Maybe nobody will come out to the ranch to see Harvey Frye. Maybe he is the only one in on this deal.

Still, he could feel the tightness inside him growing instead of easing and just telling himself to relax was evidently not good enough. The girl had covered most of the distance at a quick trot and was now drawing rein in front of the house. One of the men came out of the bunkhouse, took the reins of the nearer horse and held the animals steady as she climbed down, made to go into the house, then walked over to her father. They stood for a long while in deep and earnest conversation.

Smiling thinly to himself, he wondered whether she was telling the other about her attempt to get him to give up this trail of vengeance on which he had set himself, to ride out and leave them in peace. For a moment, he felt suddenly sorry for those two people down there, standing in the sunlight; innocent people who had been drawn into this drama through no fault of their own. Then he hard-

ened himself. This was something which had to be played
out to its finish. He had committed himself the moment
he had ridden up from Texas and there was nothing that
could stop him now except maybe a bullet in the back. His
gaze lowered, coming back along the ground, up the slope
to where he lay. Again he settled down to wait. The sun
continued to climb, marking out the minutes and spacing
them into hours. He had brought his canteen up with him
and now uncorked it and took a drink of cool water,
washed it around his mouth several times before swallowing it. Time passed slowly. As yet, he had seen no sign of
Harvey Frye. The possibility that the other might not be
down there, might be in town getting ready to stir up trouble against him, disturbed him a little.

It was less than three hours later, though actually it
seemed longer, that he saw Harvey Frye. The other came
out of the rear entrance to the ranch house, walked a
short distance away from the building and stood looking
out across the valley in Brad's direction, scanning the low
hills, almost as if he were able to push his gaze through the
distance and see him crouched there in the long, rough
grass. With a Winchester he would have been able to draw
a bead on the other, lay the sights on his chest, and drop
him without any trouble. Then, maybe, it would all be
over. Yet he would never he sure that he had killed the
right man in spite of all the evidence there seemed to be
against him. Brad's eyes stayed on the other, watching his
every move, wondering a little what the other was up to.

He shifted positions as his body became cramped. After
a while, Frye seemed to get tired of waiting and moved
back towards the house, but he did not go inside, instead
he moved around the side of the long, low building, into
the courtyard and then over to the bunkhouse, ducking
his head and stepping inside.

For a long while, everything was quiet. The heat lay on
him like a suffocating blanket and he found himself taking

frequent sips of water from his canteen. It was certainly beginning to look as though he had been wrong, thinking that Harvey Frye might be innocent, that there might be someone else in this deal.

He was there a longer time now. The sun was at its zenith and there were no shadows down in the valley. The sweat dripped from his forehead into his eyes and he tilted his hat back on his head, rubbing at the spot on his scalp where the sweat band had dug deep into his flesh, forming a red weal on the skin.

Hunger growled in his stomach but he forced himself to ignore it. He was determined to see this thing through now that he had started and his thoughts gelled in his head as he caught sight of the sudden movement out of the corner of his eye, right on the edge of his vision. Sharply, he swung his head, stared out into the sun-hazed distance where the narrow trail twisted into the trees. A man was riding out of the hills, riding slowly and cautiously, head bent low in the saddle, as though he had no wish to be seen. It was just possible that it was one of the linemen coming in from his chores at the camp, but there was something about the way in which the other rode which made Brad think otherwise.

Shielding his eyes against the vicious glare of the sun, he tried to make out who the other was. Medium height, holding himself stiffly erect even though his head was bowed forward, he did not look like a cowhand. Could it be one of the nesters, trying to ingratiate himself with Harvey Frye, in return for some favours? Could it be just another trail drifter, looking for a job?

Brad waited while the other approached the courtyard, still riding slowly, turning his head this way and that, as though looking furtively for someone. A low whistle came from the bunkhouse and Brad saw the rider wheel his mount with a sudden movement, stare in that direction for a moment, then gig his horse towards the low wooden building; throw a further quick look around the court-yard, then swing down from the saddle and go inside.

Brows knit in puzzled thought, Brad lay quite still, the burning heat of the sun on his back, the dryness of his mouth and throat forgotten. Who was this stranger who had ridden so secretively into the Frye place and had this clandestine meeting with Harvey Frye? Obviously the two of them had something of vital importance to talk over in the bunkhouse, a talk which they did not wish to have disturbed by anyone else.

It was the best part of an hour later before the man came out of the bunkhouse again, stood for a moment talking earnestly to Harvey Frye, then climbed into the saddle, leaned down to say some final words to the other before digging spurs into the animal's flanks and riding out of the courtyard a great deal faster than he had ridden in. Brad watched the cloud of dust marking the other's position as it drifted towards the hills at the bend of the trail, then lowered his gaze to where Harvey Frye was walk-ing slowly back to the ranch house. Brad rubbed the back of his hand over his lips. From where he was it looked as though it had been the stranger who had been giving the orders.

There was something here which might bear investiga-tion. Obviously, the man had ridden in from town and it might not be too difficult to find him again if he was stay-ing there. He eased his way back from the lip of the ridge to where he had left his mount, was on the point of turn-ing and getting to his feet when he heard the faint snicker from his horse.

A warning voice froze him in his tracks. 'Stay right where you are, mister. There are three rifles trained on you right now.'

A pause as he remained there in a low crouch. Then he heard the crunch of boots moving over the protruding rocks and a shadow fell over him. Glancing up, he saw the

tall, hatchet-faced man leering down at him. The rifle was
trained on him and a few moments later two more men
came into view. One of them led his horse forward by the
bridle.

'I recognize this *hombre*,' muttered one of the men. 'He
came ridin' in here yesterday like a stray dog with his tail
up, askin' questions. Guess the boss will want to see him.'

Brad felt anger and a quick disgust go through him. He
had been a fool. So interested in what was going on down
below him, that he never thought to check his rear. Now
these men had succeeded in coming up on him without a
sound, taking him completely by surprise. The two
reached down, caught him by the arms and wrenched him
upright. It had all been so simply, so easily done! There
was a savage wildness rioting inside him, urging him to
strike out at these men, sneering at him with contempt in
their eyes. But he fought the feeling down with an effort.
That was just what they were hoping he would do, to give
them the excuse they needed to use the butts of their rifles
on him before taking him down to the ranch.

'Let's go, mister,' said the first man harshly. He waved
the rifle with a threatening movement. Over his shoulder
he called: 'Better bring his horse along, Cal. A piece of
good horseflesh like that could be useful and I reckon
he'll have no use for it pretty soon.'

Brad bit hard on his lower lip as he stumbled forward,
down the steep slope towards the ranch-house, blinking
his eyes against the red-crimson glare of the setting sun.

Reaching the courtyard, the tall man said: 'Stay here,
Matt – go get the boss. Tell him what we've got here.' The
short man went inside the ranch-house, came out a couple
of minutes later with Harvey Frye at his heels. The other
walked straight over to them, glanced quickly over his
shoulder at the house, then snapped: 'Get him inside the
bunkhouse. I don't want any of the others to see him. You
understand.'

'Sure, boss.' The tall man jabbed the foresight of the rifle into Brad's midriff, thrusting him back. 'You heard what Mister Frye said, stranger. '

Slowly, Brad obeyed. He could guess that Harvey would not want his father or his sister to know he was there. Clearly, the other had something in mind for him, did not want them to know of his presence so that when his body was found – if it was ever found – there would be no awkward auestions asked by anyone.

Inside the bunkhouse, Harvey Frye settled himself down on the edge of one of the bunks and looked up at Brad, a faint, tight-lipped smile on his face. He said slowly: 'I've tried to warn you, Brad. Seems you won't take a friendly warning and now you see what happened I can't afford to let you go on plaguing me like this. If I do, it won't be too long before you stumble on the truth and that is somethin' I can't allow to happen. You understand my position, of course. This stupid feud of yours, against me, is just a small part of my worries. Whenever anything like this occurs, I always do my best to get rid of it before things really get out of hand. That's how I managed to get where I am now.'

'By being a traitor to your cause; selling secret information to the enemy and then allowing someone else to take the blame for it,' Brad said bitterly, spitting the words out at the other.

He saw the sudden tightness come to the other's face, saw the blood rush into his cheeks and then drain away almost as quickly. His words had doubtless struck the other to the core.

'You've got absolutely no proof of that,' he said finally. 'No proof at all. You're just guessing.'

'Am I? If that were so, why have you done your best to kill me? These are not the actions of an innocent man.'

'You would have ridden in here and shot me down without a chance to explain or defend myself,' retorted the other. 'That was the only reason I did that. But now it's quite obvious to me that you'll never stop. So I have to take certain steps to ensure that you cause me no further trouble.'

Brad thinned his lips. 'You'll never get away with killing me in cold blood, Frye, and you know it. Even if you do have the Sheriff in your pay, there will be questions asked in town.'

'I don't think so.' Frye was still smiling, still at his ease. 'Nobody can connect you with the Lazy J this time.'

'You think I'd be fool enough to ride out here without telling somebody where I was headed?'

'Yes,' Frye nodded. 'I do. The only man in Medicine Reach likely to know is the groom at the livery stables and it will not be difficult to silence him.'

'And how do you propose to silence me? By now, the whole of the town will know that you've already made two unsuccessful attempts to kill me. You'll be the first man they'll suspect.'

'Not if your body is never found,' said the other smoothly. 'But enough of this talk. It will be dark soon.' He turned to the three men who stood near him. 'I want you to tie his hands behind his back. Take his guns so that he won't give you any trouble, then ride with him until you're well off the spread and finish him. You understand?'

'Sure, boss,' grinned the tall man. 'We understand.'

'Good. See that there are no mistakes. We've fooled around with him for too long. I shall want to see all of you when you get back. And if there is any mistake this time, you'll be answerable to me.' He got heavily to his feet, moved towards the door. 'Keep him here until it's dark. I don't want any of the others to see him. That clear?'

The men nodded in unison. Frye made to leave, then paused, looked back at Brad. For a long moment he regarded the other thoughtfully, then said quietly: 'You know, I'm really sorry that things had to happen this way, Brad. I used to like you in the old days when we fought together. You were a damned good officer, one of the best we had.' A pause, then he went on: 'I would like you to know that you've been quite wrong in quite a lot of things. It's a pity that you couldn't have realized them before. Then this might never have occurred.'

'I still think you're a damned traitor and a coward,' Brad said harshly, spitting the words out through tightly-clenched teeth.

The other shrugged faintly, then stepped outside, closing the door behind him. Brad eyed the three men warily, decided that there was nothing to be gained by trying anything, although the thought lived for a moment in his mind. If he was to make any attempt to save his life he would have to do it when they were away from the ranch. He could not even bank on getting outside of this bunkhouse and letting the girl or her father know he was there.

'Reckon you'd better seat yourself, cowboy,' said one of the men. 'We'll be here for some little time.' As he spoke, he came forward and plucked the guns from the holsters, thrusting them into his belt. He placed the rifle against the wall at the far side of the bunkhouse, then seated himself on one of the bunks, taking it easy, but not once removing his hard-eyed gaze from Brad.

The others took up their positions near the door and after a moment's reflection Brad sat down, thoughts running riot in his head. He knew that any attempt to try to reach the door would be useless and only result in a beating from these men. If he was to have any chance at all of escape he would need all of his wits and strength about him. So he sat quietly, staring at the stove in the middle of the floor where a fire had been lit, the flames beginning to crackle along the twigs and pieces of wood which had been thrust down into it. At the moment he had one weapon which the others had not thought fit to search him for. Believing that once they had relieved him of his guns he was unarmed and helpless, they had over-looked the knife, long-bladed and keen, thrust down into his belt behind his back.

'Mind if I have a smoke?' he asked after a pause.

The tall man hesitated a moment, then hefted the rifle into his hands, said softly: 'All right, mister, but don't try any tricks or this is likely to go off and we won't need to ride out with you after dark.'

The look in his eyes told Brad that he meant every word. Digging out the tobacco and paper, he rolled himself a smoke, got slowly and carefully to his feet and went over to the stove, bending to get a light for a ciga-rette, conscious all of the time that the barrel of the rifle held in the other's hands followed him closely, a finger tight across the trigger. Straightening up, he dragged the smoke down into his lungs, went back to the bunk and sat down, springs creaking under his weight. He still cursed himself inwardly for what had happened. If he had only taken the most elementary precautions he would never have been taken by surprise like that. He had been a fool; a complete and utter fool. There was no other name for it.

Finishing the smoke, he lay back on the bunk, his hands clasped behind his head, staring up at the low ceil-ing above him. He tried to give no show of outward concern, knowing that these men were watching him closely and carefully, trying to assess for themselves the sort of person he really was.

'I'll say this for you, stranger,' murmured one of them at length. 'You're a real cool *hombre*. Here's death starin' you in the face, and you don't seem to have turned a hair.'

Brad shrugged. 'I get the impression that you're the boys who are makin' the big mistake. Oh sure, you can ride me out and shoot me in the back, try to hide my body somewhere, but sooner or later – and I figure it'll be sooner than any of you think – the Sheriff and some of the townsfolk will come ridin' out here prodding and probing until they turn up somethin' and then there'll be all hell to pay.'

The big man eyed him narrowly. 'You don't talk any kind of sense, mister,' he said, his tone harsh. The wrinkles around the corners of his eyes had deepened just a shade in sudden thought. 'Nobody will bother if you fail to turn up. You rode in from Texas, you stayed for a few weeks, and then rode out again the same way, without botherin' to tell anybody you were leavin'. Could be that you was scared away, maybe.'

Brad propped himself up on one elbow, stared straight at the other until the man's gaze slid away. 'You don't even convince yourself of that, friend,' he said.

There was no more talk. Outside, it grew steadily darker. The hunger in Brad's belly was a gnawing ache now which he could forget only with difficulty. Soon they would decide that it was dark enough for what they had to do. He watched as one of the men went to the door, opened it a crack and glanced out. Then he came back into the bunkhouse. 'Another fifteen minutes and we ride out,' he said, harshly.

Brad felt the muscles under his ribs tense at the words, but kept his face expressionless. He pushed himself upright, rubbed his neck, letting his glance move from one man to the next. Once he thought he heard move-ment outside the building, footsteps sounding in the dust, but they moved on by, fading quickly into the distance and the barrel of the rifle was laid menacingly on him, a mute warning that it would be foolish to try and cry out.

The minutes passed slowly. Then the tall man, standing near the stove, said: 'All right. On your feet, let's go!'

They all stepped closer. Brad looked quickly from face to face. None of them said anything as they motioned him towards the door. For a moment he hesitated, made as if to turn. Behind him the hammer of a gun was drawn back, the click sounding ominously loud in the clinging stillness. 'Just keep moving and do as we say,' murmured the tall man thinly, his voice little more than a hushed whisper. He stepped down from the door. His horse was tethered at the side of the bunkhouse and while he stood covered by the menacing rifle, the other two men slipped quietly across the deserted courtyard to the corral, came back a little while later with three horses already saddled. One of them swung up, unhitched his riata and made it fast to Brad's bridle, then tied it to his own saddlehorn.

'Tie his hands.' ordered the big man.

The third cowpoke came around, lashed Brad's hands together behind his back, then stood back a little, while the other struggled up into the saddle. The first time he fell, rolled quickly to one side as his horse shied at the sudden commotion, the lashing feet just missing his head as he sprawled helplessly on the ground, dust on his lips and in his mouth. At last he was in the saddle, gripping the bay tightly with his knees to retain his balance.

With two of the men leading the way and the third following close behind, they rode out of the ranch and headed towards the hill country to the north. As he rode, Brad studied the terrain around him. The hills were low, dark shapes against the star silvered night. There was no moon and in the blackness, he succeeded in flexing his fingers behind him, ignoring the thongs which cut deeply into his wrists as he gently, an inch at a time, eased the knife from its scabbard.

Staring straight ahead of him, he strained his arms to their utmost limit, knowing that it would be utterly impossible for him to saw through the thongs that bound him unless he could fasten the knife somehow, with the sharp-edged blade exposed. At any moment, too, the man riding at his back might become suspicious and move up closer, take a look at what he was doing. He felt the sweat break out on his forehead and the muscles of his back, his shirt sticking to his body, chafing it with every movement he made.

It was slow work, hampered by having to maintain his grip on the horse with his knees. Ahead of them the ground began to rise, become more stony and uneven. Desperately, he fought to keep his balance in the saddle as the trail wound up the lee of one of the towering hills.

The tall man's voice came drifting back from up ahead. 'Keep close up, Bob. This is likely to be tricky and we don't want him to go over the side and drag Vince with him.'

The man at the rear moved up, came alongside Brad, 'You heard what he said,' he snapped harshly. 'Keep that horse of yours moving.'

'I can't move much faster,' Brad said thinly. 'Untie my hands and I might be able to do so.'

The other uttered a harsh laugh. 'You take us for fools,' he snarled. He reached out and struck the bay viciously, sending it jerking forward along the stony trail. The sudden start almost threw Brad from the saddle. Grimly, he held on, sucking air into his lungs, swaying from side to side, knowing that the rocky wall on one side of the trail was only scant inches from his head, that if he swayed too far he could strike the rock wall with his skull and that could be the end of him. Somehow, he managed to regain his balance, to slow the bay to an easier pace. The man had moved a little ahead of him, but the rope still had him tied to Vince's saddlehorn.

He tightened his lips. With all of these men in front of him, this might be his only chance to cut himself free. Withdrawing the knife the whole way from the scabbard, he succeeded in jamming the hilt tightly down into the back of the saddle, the blade thrusting upward. How long he had before they grew suspicious, he didn't know. All he could do was ignore the thin stabs of agony as his wrists touched the edge of the blade, knowing that there was blood flowing warmly down between his fingers, that it needed only one slip for the knife to slice through the vein and it would not matter what happened then. The thongs were strong, resisted even the sharp blade. Sweat trickling down his cheeks in spite of the coldness of the night air, he continued to saw at the leather thongs, feeling them weaken only slowly as the knife sawed through them.

'He all right back there, Bob?' called the man up front. They were angling around a wide shoulder of rock, their horses picking their way carefully. In places the trail was less than three feet wide and there was a deepening chasm on one side, with the sheer rock wall still on the other. This made it impossible for Bob to ride back alongside him and in the darkness, Brad saw the man turn his head, his face a grey blur in the night as he peered back at him, the rope snaking back.

'I guess he won't get out of that in a hurry,' Bob called back.

'Keep your eye on him. We'll be coming down into the open meadows soon. If he tries anything, shoot him.'

'I figure there's nothin' he can try,' said Bob with a throaty laugh. He eased his mount's pace a little so that he was riding only a few feet ahead of Brad. Deliberately, moving his arms slowly, Brad sawed the thongs up and down the blade, felt them give suddenly. His hands were free, but there was no feeling in them and he held them rigidly behind his back, flexing the fingers as a million red-hot needles stabbed through his flesh with the returning circulation. Gently, he eased the knife from the saddle, held it carefully in his right hand. He would have to choose his moment carefully to cut the rope which held him to Vince's mount.

The road curved down from the hills. The rocky wall which had hemmed them in most of the way shelved down abruptly and they came out on the smoother downgrade, dipping towards the plain which lay to the north of the

Lazy J spread. In the shimmering starglow, Brad was just able to make out the fence a short distance ahead and a little while later they rode through a gap in it and struck out across more open, rugged country. A quick glance around him told him that he would have to act quickly now. They would soon reach the place where they intended to kill him and he would have to catch them off their guard if he was to have any chance at all.

Slowly, he eased himself forward in the saddle, gripping the knife tightly, not once removing his gaze from the man who rode directly ahead of him. The other had his back to him at the moment, was looking towards the dark shadow of timber that showed to their left. Brad took it all in with one swiftly encompassing glance. Then, slashing at the rope, he sliced through it, held the end briefly in his left hand so that there was no slackness in it to warn Vince, then let it go, kicked his heels into the horse's flanks, at the same time pulling it round savagely, spurring it towards the low trees.

He heard a shout behind him as one of the men yelled a warning. A shot sounded and the slug whistled past his ears as he bent low in the saddle. He knew that he had only a few yards advantage over the others, although he would have backed his horse against theirs. Ears back, head thrust forward, tail streaming out behind it, the bay sped swiftly towards the timber. If there were any gopher holes here which could prove disastrous, he could not worry about them now. All he knew was that the three men had swung off the trail and were now headed after him in pursuit.

More shots sounded, but in the darkness, with the start he had on them, taking the men completely by surprise, the shots went wide and almost before he knew it, he was in among the timber, slender branches whipping savagely across his face. The undergrowth slowed him down appreciably, but it also threw the others off the scent, would force them to split up.

Carrying on the small wind he heard Vince yell: 'Split up and ride around the timber. We'll trap him in the brush, then move in from three sides. He can't get out.'

'You're right,' called Bob, his voice coming from a slightly different direction. 'He's ridden himself into a trap. Besides, he's got no guns. He can't get away now.'

Brad listened grimly to their shouts, followed their movements, knew that two of them were working their way in opposite directions around the timber, while the third pushed in on his heels.

He knew exactly what he wanted and what he intended to do. Unknowingly, the three killers had played right into his hands. They considered him to be no longer a menace to them, that he had only the knife with which he had cut himself free, whereas they could stand off and cut him down with rifle or revolver fire. But they had been forced to split up in order to trap him here and that suited his purpose admirably.

Reaching forward he unhitched the coiled riata from where it had been lashed to the front of the saddle, ran the supple rope through his fingers as he reined his mount to a halt in a small clearing. Dropping from the saddle, he pulled the bay into the bushes and waited. He could hear the crashing of a man who was riding into the timber at his back, following his trail through the trees. He would undoubtedly be the first to reach him.

A few moments later the other came thrusting into the small clearing, reined up quickly on the edge of it, clearly apprehensive, straining his ears in an attempt to locate him. Caution was obviously riding the other, dictating his actions. The man knew that he had dismounted, was waiting somewhere in the darkness. In the gloom Brad saw him edge his mount forward very slowly, head turning from side to side. Even a man armed only with a knife could be extremely dangerous in the darkness.

Brad waited until the other was less than ten feet from

him, leaning forward in his saddle, peering into the bushes. Swiftly he whirled the riata around his head, then let it go, the rope dropping neatly over the man's shoulders as he half turned in Brad's direction. He had drawn one of his Colts from its holster, but the rope forced his arms to his side and before he could move or cry out, Brad had jerked him savagely from the saddle. The other hit the ground hard, rolled over groggily and tried to get to his feet. He succeeded only in getting to his knees as Brad ran forward, kicked the gun from the other's grasp, caught at the other weapon and jerked it free of leather. Only then did he release the rope. He said tightly: 'If you want to stay alive, I'd advise you to keep quiet. One shout from you and I'll kill you.' His tone left no doubt that he meant what he said and the other maintained a sullen, reluctant silence.

His mouth hung partly open as he sucked air into his lungs and his eyes, though staring straight ahead, were like live coals in the shadow of his face. It was the man called Bob.

A voice yelled harsh and loud from the distance. It was answered from the other side of the timber.

'Seems your friends are determined to try to hunt me down,' Brad said, his voice soft. 'When they do find me however, they're sure going to regret it.' He lifted the Colt meaningly, checked that the chambers were loaded, then reversed it without warning and brought the butt crashing down on the other's head. The man fell forward against his feet without a sound, only his breath escaping through his lips in a low, half-heard murmur.

He would be out for some time, Brad guessed. Leaving the man where he had fallen, he went over to the other side of the clearing, crouched down in the brush, straining every nerve to pick out the positions of the other two men. He could hear them vaguely m the distance but as yet they did not seem to be closing in on him.

For a few minutes it was all quiet. Then he heard the sound a horse would make as it thrust its way through waist-high bushes. Steadying himself, he peered off into the darkness, paused as he thought he caught a movement in the pines far off where the trail ran through them. He raised the Colt, finger on the trigger, sighting the weapon along the trail, waiting as the seconds passed and lengthened into minutes.

There it was again. After three minutes of utter silence, during which he guessed the two men had dismounted and were advancing cautiously on foot, he saw a figure dart forward from the trees, running a couple of yards along the trail, crouched low, keeping his head down. He went down out of sight a moment later, dropping back into the undergrowth which grew right up to the trail at that point.

Sighting on the spot where he knew the other had gone to ground, he loosed off a couple of shots. Both missed and a second later he heard a voice yell: 'Hold your fire, Bob. It's us.'

Brad grinned mirthlessly. 'Your friend is taking no further interest in this fight,' he called loudly.

'It's Calder,' he heard Vince say in a shaky tone. 'He must've got the drop on Bob. Now he's got his guns.'

'That's right. Now throw up your hands and step out nice and easy.' His words echoed in the narrowness between the trees and at the same moment the other two men made their decision. There was a sudden movement in the bushes, the spurt of orange flame tuliping in the blackness, and bullets struck through the trees close to his body. He swung sharply, feeling the draught of one of the slugs as it passed within an inch of his cheek. Vince, the third man, must have crept up closer through the trees close to his body and was now less than fifteen yards away, on his left. There was a long deadfall there and he reckoned the other was crouched down behind it. He could not see the other man, but a split second later, there was another splash of muzzle flame from the undergrowth and Brad spun round sharply, aiming at that spot now, emptying his gun straight along the trail to where the gunfire had shown. The burned powder bloomed a blue-crimson in the darkness. he heard a great shot go up in the middle of the racket, and then muzzle light leapt out at him with quick explosions as Vince fired from the other direction.

Ducking back, he lay flat on the ground, not daring to lift his head, as he carefully plucked cartridges from his belt and thrust them into the warm chambers. There came no sound from the man further along the trail and Brad guessed that one of his slugs had probably found its mark, But Vince was still around and still dangerous.

'Better come out with your hands lifted, Vince,' Brad called. 'You don't stand a chance now. These aren't the sort of odds you like, one man against the other. You only fight when there are three of you against an unarmed man.'

A shot came from a few feet from where the last ones had originated and he knew that Vince was trying to edge his way around, maybe to work his way back along the trail to where he had left his mount, to ride back with a whole skin and warn Harvey Frye that things had gone sour on them, that Brad Calder was still very much alive and the other two men were, for all he knew, dead. But in a flash of understanding, Brad knew with a sudden certainty that Vince would not do that. If he succeeded in getting out of there with a whole skin he would take his horse, and keep on riding, away from the territory. Harvey Frye had already promised what would happen if he did not carry out his orders. Vince was no fool. He would not deliberately ride back to face that kind of music if he could help it. At best, he was a renegade and a killer, and such men had, as their primary concern, their own personal welfare. There were no heroes among these men. They hunted in packs. When the moment came to face up to the fact that they were fighting on even terms with a man who could use a gun just as well as they could, they cut and run. They might fight for a winning cause, but as far as Vince was concerned, this had abruptly turned into a losing one and he wanted no more of it.

Slowly, Brad got to his feet, padded forward, cat-footed, into the dimness of the trail, keeping to the opposite side to where he knew Vince to be. He could just pick out the sound of the other's furtive movements through the brush. Even in the darkness the other was taking little care to move silently. His fear was suddenly an overwhelming force that blotted out all other considerations in his mind. All he wanted now was to get away from this scene of destruction. The unexpected suddenness with which the tables had been turned on them, had shocked him to the point where he could no longer think clearly.

He began to run, stumbling through the clawing bushes, falling against the trunks of the trees in his head-long flight. Brad caught a fragmentary glimpse of his dark figure as the other darted across an open space at the bend of the trail. He jerked up the gun from his waist and fired. The bullet missed the stumbling man by a foot, cut bark from the trunk of the tree directly ahead of him. Vince reeled back instinctively. He whirled, lifted his gun, aimed it in Brad's direction and squeezed the trigger. There were only two shots left and both went wild.

Before he had a chance to reload Brad was on him. Stung by a blind, savage anger that overrode his natural caution, angered by events which had happened to him since arriving in this territory, determined to wreak vengeance on somebody, and this gust of swift, physical reaction brought near disaster in its train. Even as he moved in, lunging forward through the brush, the other stepped to one side, hurled the empty, useless gun at him.

The weapon struck him on the side of the head, a hard, powerful blow. An inch to the right and it would have ended the fight there and then. As it was, Brad felt as if paralysis had struck. All of the strength and feeling ran from his body in a single moment and it was a miracle that he was able to remain on his feet. There was a roaring in his ears and a blackness shot through with stars in front of his eyes. Air refused to go down into his heaving, aching lungs and he closed desperately with the other as the man tried to ram piston-like blows into his face and chest. Wrestling, recovering his balance, Vince tried to pull himself clear, to leave room for a damaging blow while he still held the advantage. Brad clung to him tenaciously, forced to take several numbing blows on his neck and shoulders in the process. But gradually, he was able to breathe again and think clearly. He had almost made a fatal mistake. Now the pent-up anger had released itself and strength and co-ordination began to take its place.

Madly, Vince hauled him out on to the trail. Feet scrabbling in the tangle of grass and upthrusting roots, he rushed Brad backwards, intending to smash him against the trunk of one of the tall trees, using all of his weight and strength to crush him there, force him to release his smothering hold. Brad saw it coming, deliberately let his legs go under him, bracing his shoulders for the shock of hitting the ground hard, pulling at Vince's jacket with all of his force as he went over backwards. The killer, unable to halt his headlong rush went flying over Brad's prone body.

Pushing himself to his feet, the hair falling over his face and into his eyes, Brad set himself as the other rolled over, half stunned by the impact of the fall. Vince was more wary now. Dazed and with a look of disbelief on his face, he stalked forward, head lowered. Brad waited for him, his fists bunched tightly by his sides. With a deep-throated growl of anger the other launched himself across the trail, head down, meaning to butt him in the stomach and send him down again.

Side-stepping the other's blind, impetuous rush, Brad slammed a fist into the other's side and as Vince rocked back, clubbed him with both clenched fists on the back of the neck. A thinned whistle came from between the other's teeth as he fell forward, unable to help himself. Brad went forward, merciless. Vince was muttering something under his breath, one of his eyes half-closed, his lips puffy. He was almost out on his feet, yet some animal instinct forced him to bend and cover up his vital parts, arms crossed over his body, backing away a little until he reached the end of the trail and stood there, wavering, teetering on his feet.

He swung a feeble blow at Brad as the other stepped forward and although it landed on its mark, there was no strength behind it and Brad scarcely felt it. Putting in another teeth-snapping blow to Vince's chin, he felt the other's head jerk back on his shoulders, knew that the man was almost finished.

Grabbing him by the shirt, bunching the cloth in his fist, he said harshly: 'Now you're going to answer a few questions, Vince. Any lies and I'll finish this little job. You understand?'

There was a flicker of defiance in the other's narrowed eyes. 'You'll get nothin' out of me,' he mumbled through smashed lips.

'We'll see about that,' Brad grated. 'First, I want to know why Harvey Frye is so goddamned anxious to have me killed. Second, who was that stranger who rode into the Lazy J this afternoon for a secret pow-wow with him.'

'I don't know what you're – talking about,' grunted the other. 'I saw nobody there today.'

'Seemed to me they knew each other pretty well from the way they acted.' Brad tightened his grip, drew back his other fist. 'You going to talk now, or do I have to pistol-whip you?'

'I tell you I don't know anythin'. Why don't you ask Frye if you're so anxious to know?'

Brad grinned mirthlessly. 'He doesn't seem to want to talk for some reason. He prefers to send three of his paid killers to get rid of me.'

Vince tried a weakly pawing swing which Brad caught on a hunched shoulder and with a short, jabbing right he dropped the other again. Vince lay in a huddled heap at his feet, his head lolling against the trunk of the tree, moaning softly under his breath as he tried feebly to rise.

This man had had his share of trouble, of rough and tumble, but never before had he been hit by blows like this. He knew that he had now come up against his match, that he would go on getting hit until he told this man what he wanted to know.

Bending, Brad pulled him to his feet again. 'I'm only going to ask you once more. Harvey Frye told you to kill me. Why?'

'He said that you meant to kill him no matter what happened. That you were somebody from his past who'd sworn to kill him. He first tried to warn you off, but you stuck around in Medicine Reach and he began to realize that this was the only way to fix you.'

'That the only reason he wants me dead?' Brad continued remorselessly.

'I don't know,' mumbled the other. 'Leave me be.' There was something in the man's voice, in the shifty stare of his eyes which told Brad he was lying, that he knew more than he was telling. He slapped the other swiftly over the jaw with the flat of his hand, lips drawn back mirthlessly from his teeth.

'I won't ask you again.'

'He —' The other paused, lifted his right hand and rubbed it across his smashed face, staring down at the smear of blood with a kind of morbid fascination. Then he

looked up again into the pitiless face of the man who
stood above him. 'He had to do this,' Vince said finally.

Brad nodded his head slowly, beginning to see a glim-
mer of truth. 'That man who rode in today. Was he the
one who gives the orders?'

'Yes,' Vince nodded.

'When did he first show?'

'About a month back,' muttered the other. 'He just
rode into the ranch one morning and asked to see the
boss. When Harvey Frye saw him, I guessed it was something bad. They went into a huddle for quite a while.'

'You know what they were talking about?' Brad
demanded.

The other shook his head. 'Must have been somethin'
about you,' he said at length.

'Why do you say that?'

The other licked his lips. 'It was just after that, Harvey
Frye told us all to be on the look out for a stranger who
would be riding up from the south. He told us what he'd
look like and that description sure fitted you, mister.'

Slowly, Brad nodded. He released his hold on the
other's shirt and Vince slid down the trunk of the tree, his
legs going from under him. Brad stood quite still for a
long moment, staring down at the other, then wheeled
and walked back into the clearing, catching his mount.
Bob still lay where he had fallen, arms flung out in front
of him, legs doubled up beneath his unconscious body.
There would be no further trouble from either of these
two men he thought fiercely. They had failed in what they
had set out to do and if he knew their type, once they
came round, they would catch their mounts and ride on
out of the territory; and the Lazy J would not see either of
them again. He felt reasonably certain that they would not
even run the risk of warning Harvey Frye of what had
happened, that the man they had been instructed to kill
was still on the loose.

Riding out of the clearing, he glanced up at the star strewn sky, guessed that it was close on midnight, and set his mount along the trail to the south. Now was the time to have things out with Harvey Frye, he decided. There were questions which the other would have to answer.

He reached the hills overlooking the Lazy J ranch shortly before dawn and sat his mount, smoking thoughtfully, watching the late stars fading as the grey flush began to brighten slowly. A faint dampness hung in the air and he pulled the high collar of his jacket up around his neck, studying the layout of the terrain before him. Harvey Frye would not be expecting him to ride back. Maybe at that very moment he would be down there, waiting anxiously for his three killers to return with news of his demise. A tiny gust of anger boiled through him at the thought. Even if Frye was not the man he sought, the man who had branded him a coward had been responsible for the deaths of nine good men, he still had something for which to answer. But that day of reckoning could wait until he had finished the job he had come here to do, unless Frye wanted to push his luck and did something rash when they met face to face.

Slowly the dawn brightened. The last of the stars vanished. There was a red glow building up in the east, touching the clouds which lay in a long, dark bar across the heavens close to the horizon.

A light showed in one of the windows of the ranchhouse and a little later, a group of men came from the bunkhouse, washed themselves at the pump in the yard, then went over for breakfast. He waited until they had finished their meal and most of them had ridden out to their daily chores, before raking spurs along his horse's flanks and putting it to the downslope. He rode into the dusty courtyard, the hollow sound of hoofbeats preceding him. Reining up, he waited as the door opened and Harvey Frye rushed out. Before the other had a chance to

take in who it was and go for his gun, Brad levelled the
weapon he had taken from the killer, his finger steady on
the trigger.

'I don't want to kill you, Harvey,' he said thinly, 'but if
you make me, I will.'

He saw the shocked disbelief in the other's eyes. The
man was literally frozen by astonishment. Keeping the
Colt trained on the other, Brad slid from the saddle,
walked forward until he stood in the courtyard immediately below the other.

'I guess you didn't expect to see me again, Harvey,' he
said tautly. 'Trouble is, you should never trust anybody to
do your dirty work for you. If you want to be certain, you
have to do it yourself. Now if you care to step down into
the yard, we can settle it here and now. If not, then there
are some things you'd better tell me.'

Harvey Frye opened his mouth to speak, but at that
moment there was another movement and Janet Frye
appeared in the doorway. Her glance swept over the two
men, watching them closely. Then she said quickly, her
words a rush of sound, 'Put up that gun, Brad. If there's
some reason for this, I'm sure that we can sort it out without gunplay.'

Brad shrugged then, deliberately, he holstered the gun.
'It seems that your brother is slow to learn, Ma'am,' he
said tightly, his words dropping into a sudden, muffling
silence. 'He tried to have me killed last night. Reckon I've
got a right to know why before I decide on what to do.'

Janet Frye swung on her brother, her eyes wide. 'Is this
true, Harve?' she asked tautly. Her gaze locked with his. 'Is
it?'

'Of course not,' said the other uneasily. He lowered his
glance, as though unable to meet hers. 'Why should I want
to kill him? He means nothing to me.'

Janet Frye turned to Brad, her lips pressed close into a
tight line. 'What's your version of this, Brad?'

'It's quite simple. Three of your men jumped me up yonder on the hill and brought me down here, kept me in the bunkhouse until it was dark so that nobody else would know I was there. Harvey gave them implicit orders to ride me out once it was dark and kill me someplace, so long as it was off the spread and nobody could connect my death with the Lazy J. Unfortunately, those killers were a trifle careless. Somehow, they lost me in the darkness.

'One of them is dead, the other two are still alive, although a little the worse for wear and if needs be I figure they can be still made to talk. One did talk.' He threw a sharp-bright stare at the man who stood near the wooden upright on the porch.

'He's lyin',' called Harvey urgently. He spread his hands wide. 'There are no killers. If what he said was true, he would have brought them back here. But he can't produce them, can you, Calder?'

'I guess the Sheriff will have them by now,' Brad said slowly. He had an idea that the other was stretched close to breaking point, that given enough rope, he would betray himself.

'I believe him, Harve,' said the girl sharply.

'And so do I,' said a harsh voice from just inside the house. Brett Frye came out on to the porch. His hair shone greyly in the dawn light. There was a hard expression on his weather-beaten face. 'I've suspected that there was something like this for quite some time. You've never been the same since you came back from the war. Something changed you from the man who went away to fight for the South. I reckon it's time we knew the truth.'

Harvey Frye's face was a hard mask. His eyes stared from one to the other like those of a trapped animal. Then his shoulders slumped fractionally and Brad knew that the other was beaten.

'All right,' he said slowly, his voice just a strained whisper. 'I'll tell you.' He still hesitated, then went on hoarsely:

'I had to do this. I had no other choice. If I hadn't, I would have been killed.'

'That stranger who rode in to see you yesterday?' Brad interrupted.

'So you did see him.' Slowly, tiredly, Frye nodded. 'You've probably guessed by now that he was the man who betrayed you and the others to the enemy. I found out but he threatened that he would kill me, if you didn't, and forced me to keep quiet. I figured that so long as you were in Texas, a thousand miles or so away, there would be no trouble. But you started riding north, looking for me. Oh, I heard about that and I knew why you were coming. I reckoned that if I could steer you away without too much trouble, everythin' would be all right. But you refused to be steered. That's when he threatened to provide "evidence" which would prove conclusively that I was the traitor. He said he'd see that you got the evidence and once that happened it would be the end of me. The only other alternative was for me to ensure that you were removed.'

'So when I fell into your hands you were determined to make sure of it.'

'I had to. There was no other way out. He has men with him now, renegades from the hills.'

'And you know where he is now?'

'I guess he could be anywhere,' said the other listlessly. All of the fight seemed to have been beaten out of him. Now he was merely a man, whipped and without pride.

'Come now,' Brad said tonelessly, 'you can do better than that. Where is he?'

'If you know anythin' at all, I think you owe it to Mister Calder to tell him,' said Brett Frye tersely. 'You've caused enough trouble already. This is maybe your only chance to redeem yourself in some small way.'

'He's got a hideout up in the hills.'

'Where?' muttered Brad relentlessly.

'Up near Clearwater Springs. There's a valley there. But you don't stand a chance if you're thinkin' of ridin' up there after him. They can see the trail for a couple of miles in any direction. You'd be blasted from the saddle long before you got anywhere near them.'

'Maybe so,' Brad nodded tersely. 'But there's a score I've got to settle with this *hombre*.'

'Be careful he doesn't settle it with you first,' warned the other tonelessly.

Brad turned back to where his mount stood patiently in the warming rays of the rising sun. He had almost reached it when Janet Frye called: 'Won't you stay for breakfast, Brad? It's the least we can do after what has happened.'

Brad hesitated, then turned. 'I'd sure appreciate that,' he nodded. 'Didn't have a bite to eat yesterday.' He glanced up at Harvey Frye as he went into the house, but the other was not looking at him. Brad felt certain now that he had nothing more to fear from the other. Perhaps he should have called him out, exacted retribution for what he had done. But now, for some strange reason, he felt no animosity towards the other. Harvey had merely been a weak-willed pawn in the hands of someone more unscrupulous, more iron-willed.

He washed the dust from his face and arms at the sink, then sat down at the table while he ate ravenously. Across from him, Brett Frye sat deep in thought, his face lined and troubled.

At length, when the last morsel had been eaten and he sat back sipping the hot coffee, feeling better than he had for more than twenty-four hours, the older man said: 'I don't know how we can atone for what my son did, Mister Calder. I can understand a lot of things now which have been puzzling me for a long time. I can only say that Harvey got caught up in something bigger and more ruthless than he is. Now he's been forced to pay the price for that. In the process you seem to have been threatened.'

'Forget it, sir,' Brad said. 'I understand. I'm glad, too, for your sakes, that Harvey wasn't the traitor. Not that it means much now. The war is over and as you say, life has to go on and we must try to build something better and more enduring than that which went before. But for some of us the war will never be finished, until we've cleared the stain on our names.'

'You're determined to go after this man?'

'I've got to. There's no other way out for me.'

'And if you do meet him and manage to kill him? What then? Ride on over the hill, taking the trail so many angry men like you seem to take once you've killed men.'

The other laid his glance on Brad like the edge of a Bowie knife, strangely motionless, and yet ready to cut.

'I'm not sure. I reckon I'll have to cross that bridge when I come to it. This is something that has been with me for so long that I've never stopped to think of anythin' else. Maybe when it's all over and I can feel clean again, and can look a man straight in the face without wondering what he's thinking about me, there'll be time enough to consider what I can do with my life.'

'There'll always be a place here for you,' said Janet Frye slowly. She looked at her father as she spoke, and the other hesitated for only a fraction of a second before nodding his head in agreement.

Brad stood up. 'Thanks for the meal and the offer of a job,' he said. He threw a quick glance through the window at the harsh sunlight streaming down into the courtyard. It was going to be another hot, blistering day.

At the door, he paused: 'This Clearwater Springs,' he murmured. 'Where would I find it?'

'Half a day's ride from here,' said Brett Frye, rousing himself. 'Almost due west. You'll spot the hills in a couple of hours. The trail runs right through them, but about a mile into the hills there's a stone column. You leave the main trail there and cut up right into the shoulders of the hills. Clearwater Springs are at the top of that trail. But like Harvey said, they'll have posted lookouts all the way along the road. You'll be spotted long before you get there.'

'No other way in?' Brad inquired. 'Could I circle around the hills and come in from the other direction?'

'Not a chance. The valley is shut in on three sides by unscaleable ledges. You'd never make it. Least that would happen, your horse would break its leg. Much too risky even to think about.'

Brad shrugged. Near the table the girl watched him go cold, keen. 'Maybe he'll come riding here soon to see Harvey. You could get him then.'

'No. He might be expecting that. I've got to take him when he doesn't expect it. Besides, I figure I've waited too long already to finish this business. It's got to be now.'

5

EXECUTION BY GUNFIRE

The sun lifted, glared down over the wide, rolling country. Brad reached the end of the meadows and ran on between tall hedges of black pine. The sun winked at him redly through the trunks, flashing in his eyes. Now and then he deliberately pulled his mount to a walk for a breathing spell, but he felt tensed, hating the delay, scarcely able to abide it. Now that he was so close to his goal there was the tight restlessness bubbling in him once more, dominating every thought and action. Harvey Frye had not said who this man was. He may not even have known his real identity. But soon now, he would find out for himself. He would meet the man who had branded him traitor and coward, who had been the cause of his dishonour, his disownment by his family and friends. That was almost too much to be wiped clean by the death of one man, but that was how it would have to be.

The hands which held the reins were heavy across the backs and he rode tall and easy in the saddle, driven on now by his desperate urge and desire to face up to this man. He thought back several times as he rode, to the glimpse he had had of him in the glaring sunlight from the top of the hill overlooking the Lazy J ranch. Had there been anything familiar about the other, he pondered thoughtfully, any little characteristic that could give him a clue as to the man's identity? He must have been someone at regimental headquarters, otherwise he could not have got his hands on that vital information. Yet the man had certainly not been the other suspect; Colonel Weekes. Even if the other were still alive, he could not have ridden a horse as that man had done, would not have been able to exert this dominating influence over Harvey Frye.

After a while he gave up thinking along these lines, when his thoughts led to nothing. He turned his mind to the task which lay ahead of him. He did not know how many men had to be dealt with and he would have to wait until he came within sight of the place before deciding whether to wait for dark before he moved in.

Coming out of the sheltering trees he rode west into rougher, more inhospitable country, an orange-yellow flatness from which isolated buttes lifted, worn and fluted by long ages of wind and abrading dust. The stifling heat of the midday sun beat down on his back and shoulders, touched the shiny metal rings which held his gear to the saddle with swift, hurting flashes of fire. An hour later he was in the desert and there was the hot alkaline taste of the dust in his mouth, choking and sickening. Not only in his mouth, but forming a mask over his face and working its way into the folds of his skin, it burned and irritated.

By early afternoon the dust devils had begun chasing him and the conviction grew in his mind that this was going to be a more terrible day than any he had known since reaching Medicine Reach. Squinting through the shivering heat haze that lay over the vast wastelands, he could just make out the hills on the skyline. It had been called a desert because there was no water here, only the dry, arid dust, a desolation that stretched for one burning, blistering mile after another, shimmering under the fierce sun. Sitting straight in the saddle, his lips pressed tight against the infiltrating dust, his body tensed, all of his mind narrowed down to one needle point of feeling, the knowledge that now, after all these years, he was very close to killing a man who had destroyed him more surely than if he had taken a gun and put a bullet into his brain. Deep inside he felt a strange pleasure at the thought. This man was going to die slowly and watch his death approach, know just why he was dying and who it was who sent him into eternity.

It was this thought which made it possible for him to ignore the pain and the discomfort of that long ride across the desert, to ride unfeelingly when his throat was parched with thirst and his stomach rumbled painfully from hunger. His water bottle was still three-quarters filled, but he did not drink from it. It was as if his body now no longer needed these necessities for life to be sustained in it. He was nothing more than a shell of a man during that long, sun-searing afternoon, a shell that encompassed a terrible hatred.

All of his anger, all of the tension and exhaustion that had been with him all the way from Texas, was now concentrated into the burning desire to find this man, to exact from him justice and retribution. He could think of nothing else as the blazing disc of the sun lowered from its zenith and continued the long slide down the blue-white mirror of the cloudless heavens towards the horizon in front of him. He was still too far from the foothills for anyone to recognize him even if they had seen his dust. As yet, he felt little apprehension. The hooves of his mount were stirring drumbeats in his ears and for long moments, it was as if he were back in that tangle of green under-growth, listening to the Yankee bullets chirruping through the brush all around him, hearing the savage reports of the rifles, the faint cries of men as they died, feeling again the anger and the utter helplessness of the situation.

With a conscious mental effort he pulled himself back from the delusion. That was all past and done with. Nothing could bring those men back but now he had the chance to see that they, as well as himself, were avenged. A man who could betray his own kind to the enemy, deserved to die. He turned that thought over in his mind, knew a moment's hesitation. There were, of course, those who maintained that spying was a reputable profession in time of war. Maybe this man was a Yankee himself, only carrying out his orders and doing his duty. There had, after all, been Confederate spies in the Northern forces who had obtained valuable information for his own side. But that did not alter the situation as he saw it. He thrust that idea into the background of his mind and refused to consider it again. Nothing was going to sway him from his course.

Slowly, his shadow lengthened behind him as the sun lowered and a cooling finger seemed to probe through the dusty, clinging heat, cooling his brow a little. He licked his cracked, dusty lips, rubbed them with the back of his hand. As he turned north, moving towards the far edge of the hills, a little breeze sprang up, blowing into his face and except for the faint crackle of it as it sighed through the clumps of mesquite and cactus, a vast stillness lay over everything and riding had become a dull sound, with the monotony of the drumming hoofbeats in the shifting dust and the buzzing of the swarms of flies which had appeared as if from nowhere, borne on the breeze, gathering about him.

Half an hour later, with the sun just touching the rim of the hills, he crossed the edge of the desert, entered an area of broken brush and coarse, tufted grass, climbing towards higher ground. The trail he had been following earlier, angled away from him, entered the timber and vanished from sight. If Brett Frye had been right, it would continue through the trees for another mile before the point was reached where the narrower trail up to Clearwater Springs led into the higher reaches of the hills. Scanning the area ahead of him, he had already decided to try for the other direction, to seek a way up through the ledges and down into the valley from the north. It was possible that the old man had been right about this too, that there was no way in, but it was a risk he had to take.

He was nearing the crest of a long, low ridge when he heard the unmistakable sound of riders among the timber. Swiftly he touched spurs to the bay, not wanting to be out in the open if those riders came down from the hill trail. As he went down the far side of the rise he threw a quick glance over his shoulder, his sharp eyes catching a glimpse of the small bunch of riders, spurring hell for leather away from the trail, over the rougher, uneven ground and then on into the desert. In the dimness of approaching night it was impossible to guess how many there were, but he guessed at least six, possibly nearer a dozen. They rode tightly bunched together; and even as he wondered who they were and what their business had been in these hills, they had passed over a low rise and were gone from sight, only the faintly luminous cloud of dust hanging in the still air to give indication of their passing.

Twilight came on, lingered briefly, then gave way to dark. In the clear heavens the stars came out brilliantly and there was a scratch of yellow moon over to the west, giving a little additional light; just enough for him to see by, but not to make out small details. He reached a flat stretch between two tall banks of rock and set his mount to a steady canter. Mountain air blew cold against his face, congealing the sweat that lay on his back, his shirt sticking to his ribs.

As he rode, he thought more of the man he had come to kill. Once he came face to face with him, he would deliberately strip him of all his self-respect and manhood, would force him to grovel in the dirt until he stood naked of every shred of decency and hated himself for what he was – a traitor and a coward. Every waking hour, Brad had thought of this moment, but he had only just begun to consider how it was to be done. There was a sense of greedy eagerness in him now, driving him forward into the darkness of the night, oblivious to the bruises in his body.

He was a couple of miles along the narrow, partly obliterated trail when he felt the hills crowd in on him from both sides and in front of him, the trail moved steeply upgrade until it became little more than a deer track, invisible in the clinging darkness. Here he was forced to let the bay pick its own pace, placing one foot carefully in front of the other. The first wrong move and they could both be killed, hurled over the side and down on to the jagged rocks which lay a hundred feet below.

The cliff race was rock and dirt with very little vegetation growing out of it. Few plants could thrust down their roots and suck up the moisture they needed from the thin layer of topsoil which provided the only nutrition for them. Now the narrow rutted trail moved tight against the cliff, so close that he fouled his leg against out-thrusting fingers of stone. The horse was weary and doubtful. It obviously did not like this trail. Even in broad daylight it would have been difficult to make his way along it, but at night, it was a dozen times more dangerous, more treacherous.

Maybe he should, after all, have listened to Brett Frye. If this trail was truly impassable, he was not only risking his life, he was wasting precious time. The only thing he could possibly gain by going this way was the advantage of surprise. He felt certain that these outlaws would not have men watching this route into the valley. They would not believe that anyone could make it and it had been this thought which had prompted him to try it. He lifted himself a little in the saddle, reining the bay to a standstill, peering about him in the dimness. The land, he soon saw, was deceptive. There must surely be a better way off this upthrusting shoulder and down into the valley which, he guessed, lay to his left. One end of the ledge was probably anchored to the desert far behind him, with the other lifting to its greatest height at the northern end of this range of hills. But as it grew darker, with the moon setting behind the looming bulk of the hills, he began to wish that he could find some way to cut away to his left, even if it meant climbing that steep wall of rock which barred him from his destination.

He switched his glance from side to side as he edged slowly forward, the reins held slackly in his hands. His eyes were now accustomed to the darkness and it was ten minutes later as he moved cautiously around a sharply-angled bend in the narrow deer-trail, that he saw the faint scar of a track which led off to his left, angling up and round a high peak. From the look of it he judged that the trail had not been used for many years, was in places possibly little more than a foothold cut out of the solid rock. Perhaps the deer and mountain goats would be able to use it with immunity, but how would a horse and rider fare if they tried to go up it?

Hesitating for a long moment in quiet deliberation, he followed the course of the track until he could see it no longer as it swept around the base of the tall rocky pinnacle. It was his only route. If he stuck to the other trail – which was almost as dangerous in the dark – it might simply lead him around the hills and out into the desert far to the north. Morning would find him still many miles from his destination.

So it was that, not entirely free from doubt, he drew tight on the reins and put the bay to the steep upgrade. It dug in its forelegs as he had anticipated, not wishing to take the trail. Maybe it recognized the danger more clearly than he did, but he pressed it on with a touch of the rowels. In places the track pitched upwards at such an angle that he was forced to dismount and lead the animal forward, clambering over loose rocks which went bounding down the slope behind them, the crashing echoes shrieking through the stillness.

They rose up the side of the cliff in short, switchback courses. No sooner were they out of one canyon, angling around the rocky wall, than they found themselves in another. The wind sighed more strongly now, sweeping down from the summits, soft but cold against his body. In front of him now there was a long smooth plateau that stretched away into the blackness, with no vegetation growing on the surface, a curiously mounded stretch of ground, like a run of long-cooled lava that had spilled from the mouth of some volcano. He was still pointed to the upper reaches of the high hills, still a little uncertain now of whether he was heading for the valley but content to follow this track for the time being until he reached more open country, where he could take his bearings.

He had gone a hundred yards through the looming shoulders of the enveloping hills when his horse stopped. Leaning forward in the saddle, he peered into the darkness, striving to push his vision through the mantle of blackness that lay around him, to see the cause for his animal's behaviour. When he realized that his eyes had failed him, he got down and walked cautiously forward, thought he could see the trail stretching away in front of him, then bent and realized that a slide of earth and rock had come down the hillside at this point and almost completely obliterated the track. He thrust his fingers into the dirt and stones, heaving them to one side. They moved easily, were not hardpacked as he had feared, but a moment's contemplation told him that it would take him far too long to move the dirt sufficiently to clear the track. He felt the full weight of the inky shadows of the canyon pressing on him and sat idle for a moment, contemplating the position. It might just be possible that he could work a way around it. Fortunately here the track was a little wider than in most other places, and it was well away from the steep drop which had been on his left almost the whole of the way up.

Going forward, a step at a time, he explored the track as far as he could. The slide did not go back more than a couple of yards and there was a narrow space on the left where it would just be possible to squeeze through, if his luck held. He went back, spoke softly and soothingly to the horse as he caught at the bridle and led it forward. The bay was uncertain, afraid. It hauled back as he tried to budge it, resisted him. The other was a sure-footed brute, but now made wary by his experiences on the upgrade track. When he finally reached the edge of the dirt slide, he stopped again. Brad stepped up close to his head, patted the animal's nose, then moved back slowly.

'Come on, boy, you can make it.' he said reassuringly. Still the bay hesitated as Brad hauled suggestively on the bridle. When it still refused to come, he let the horse lower its head so that it might see the track. It emitted a blast of air through its nostrils, then edged forward, thrusting against him, almost taking him off balance. The next few minutes were a nightmare of stumbling, uneasy movements. The horse's flanks rubbed against the rock and he murmured gently to it to keep it from sudden, lunging panic, which could easily result in both of them going over the side, down to their deaths on the rocks far below.

Then they were around the slide and back on the continuation of the track. Here, Brad noticed with a faint sense of relief, it had broadened appreciably and he tightened the cinch, feeling the horse trembling as it stood quite still. The wind was blowing more strongly now, scouring down the face of the canyon. Taking off his hat he rubbed the back of his hand over his forehead, felt the film of sweat there, greasy under his touch. There was salt too on his lips where the sweat had dripped down his face. Getting up into the saddle, he urged the bay forward, moving slowly now, guessing that the track would sooner or later lead him into the northern end of the valley.

Around him fresh night sounds lifted and fell; a dull murmuring that made him uneasy. He could not get out of his mind that bunch of riders who had left the hills and spurred away over the desert in such a goddamned hurry. It could have been that Harvey Frye had sent word through to this man that their plan had failed for a third time, that Brad Calder was riding the trail, looking for him, and the outlaws had ridden out in the hope of cutting him off and taking him out there, in the desert before he had a chance to reach the hills.

If that were so, then he was merely wasting his time here unless he got to their camp and holed up, waiting for their return. He swung his head slowly at the sounds which lifted from the night all around him. He could see nothing and the sounds were indistinguishable. They would have been the echoes of men talking, he thought to himself; but on the other hand, they were probably nothing more than the vague murmurings of the river somewhere off in the distance, sounds which had been distorted and broken into isolated fragments by the shrouding rock walls here in the higher reaches of the hills.

The trail soon played out through thick gravel and large chunk of rock and he was on the downgrade once more. The looming hills receded into the distance, the ground opened up in front of him and he knew, without being able to see clearly, that he had reached the northern end of the valley. He could hear the river clearly now. Its bubbling roar sounded in the near distance and five minutes after reaching the open ground, he came upon the bank, where the gravel shelved down into the swift-flowing water. Freshly born in these hills, the river ran swift but shallow and entering the water, he pointed the bay upstream for better footing. The current swept hard against them, broke at the horse's legs and at the halfway point where the river bed fell steeply away, the foaming press of the current came up to the animal's chest and the bay struggled on the slippery rocks, came once to a full pause to regain its balance, then moved on again, angling to the far bank, working its way through the shallows to dry land. There were trees growing here right down to the water's edge and gaining their shelter, he dismounted, edging through the thick tangle of vines and creepers, until he came out on the other side.

In the shimmering starlight he was able to see where the tall hills rolled majestically on either side of the long, narrow valley. It was perhaps three quarters of a mile in length and perhaps a quarter of a mile wide and scanning it, he saw that Brett Frye had been almost completely right when he had said the place was virtually impregnable.

Harvey Frye had said that this man had a hideout here. He started looking for it. Being able to watch the trail for several miles, it was unlikely that they would have hidden their living quarters. Cautiously he moved forward through the darkness, one of the Colts drawn, ready for use. He saw no movement until he reached a clump of thick brush and crouched down behind it, peering ahead of him. Then the shadow moved less than fifty yards away and peering into the dark night, Brad made out the loose outline of a building of some kind, a shack he guessed, pushed up hard against the rocks at that point.

So that was where they had their hideout. The tightness grew in his body so that it was almost unbearable. He was forced to lie quite still for a long moment until he could relax a little. Then, slowly, he inched his way forward. A moment later his outstretched hand touched something soft and yielding. Instantly, he drew back, holding the gun in front of him, finger hard on the trigger. When the body in the shadows did not move, he felt again. The man lay slumped limply against one of the bushes. There was no pulse beat in his wrist and his flesh was cold. Turning him over, Brad saw the wide stain on the front of his shirt, the gun which had fallen from his lifeless fingers, lying in the grass. For a moment his mind refused to grasp the full significance of this. Then he narrowed his gaze, moved around the dead man and worked his way slowly in the direction of the shack, making no sound. He could just hear a faint crackling in the near distance and lifting his head, smelled the smoke which came drifting down the wind towards him.

There was a fire burning in the shack, he realized. Evidently somebody was still here. Ten yards further on he came across the body of another man, huddled in a vee between a couple of rocks. There was a small hole between his eyes and his rifle lay beside him where it had fallen. For a long moment he lay there in debate with himself. Those men he had seen riding away in such a hurry. Had they been the cause of this? It was beginning to look as though the outlaws' scout system had broken down, or those men had taken them completely by surprise. And the man he had ridden all this way to find? Had he been killed in the shooting, or was he inside the cabin at that very moment, maybe planning his revenge on those who had sought to destroy him that night?

It's my turn now, he thought fiercely to himself, remembering the men who had ridden under his command that time all those years ago. Men who now were buried in that isolated, lonely wood somewhere far to the south. It was as if the memories of that hillside and this quiet valley, spanning many miles and years of distance and time, had become fused in his mind. He found a kind of footing on the rough ground and worked around to the cabin. The smell of woodsmoke was stronger now and he thought he heard the faint murmur of voices from inside the place.

Edging forward, he paused some yards from the cabin, now able to make out the faint red glow of firelight that showed through the single, dusty window. Then, abruptly, he heard a shout, clean and hollowly echoing. Swiftly, he glanced up, saw the man who stood on a low rise perhaps two hundred yards away, clearly visible against the skyline. The man brought a rifle up sharply to his shoulder and fired in almost the same instant. The bullet struck close to Brad's position and he scuttled back into the brush, crouching low down as there came a sudden sound from inside the cabin. The next moment, the door was thrown open and two men came out, revolvers drawn, peering around them.

The man on the rise was running down in their direction. As he came up to the men he said loudly: 'There's another of the critters. I'm sure I saw him over that way.'

He pointed to where Brad had been a few moments before.

'Did you hit him?'

'Not sure. May have done. Saw him sneakin' up on the cabin.'

Moving slowly and quietly, Brad eased himself back into the deeper shadows, slithered down a rough slide into a wrinkle in the ground where he was temporarily out of sight from the hut, then ran along it to the far end, reached a point where bushes grew right down to it, and darted, doubled-over, into the brush, circling quickly around the cabin. In the near distance he could hear the three men moving around as they spread out, trying to locate him in the darkness. When he had reached a point on the other side of the cabin, he crouched down, listening intently.

The first man's voice called sharply: 'Any sign of him over there, Clarke?'

'Nobody here,' called another voice from further away. 'I guess you must've been firin' at shadows. All of those coyotes rode off after they jumped us.'

'No damnit! There was somebody there, I'll swear to it. He dodged back into the shadows when I spotted him and yelled a warnin'. You ought to have seen him when you came out of the but. '

'We saw nobody,' said a third voice, speaking from somewhere close to the cabin.

Brad stiffened inwardly. Where had he heard that voice before. It seemed oddly and frighteningly familiar and yet he could not place it. Maybe, he thought after a moment, it was just that it sounded like somebody he had known in the past. Memory could play funny tricks with a man, especially at times like this.

He put his thoughts to his present situation. It was not going to be so easy taking these men by surprise now that they had been alerted. But at least, some good had come of it. He knew how many there were, and where they were. 'I reckon you must've been wrong,' said the man near the hut. 'We're all jumpy tonight. None of that bunch would hang around in the valley. Those who're still alive will be ridin' back to town. We won't see their heels for dust. You'd better get back to your post just in case anyone does come sneakin' around here.'

'Who're you expectin', boss?' asked Clarke.

'Nobody. It's just that I don't want to take any chance, that's all.' There was a note of testiness in the other's tone.

'You sure that *hombre*, Calder, won't come ridin' into the hills lookin' for you?' asked the third man. Out of the corner of his vision, Brad saw him come into the open some two hundred yards away, moving towards the other two men holding a rifle in his hand.

'I told you before that Calder is dead. We don't have to worry about him any longer.'

'I reckon Clarke and me never did have to worry none,'

said the other thinly. 'After all, he's got nothin' on us. He
ain't no lawman. All he's after is the man who did him
wrong all those years ago. You ain't stopped tellin' us
about it since we've been ridin' with you. Can't say I blame
him in a way.'

'Will you shut up,' snarled the other. 'I've already told
you. Harvey Frye will do exactly as I tell him. Calder will be
dead by mornin' if he isn't dead already. And there ain't
any way he could know about this place, so put him out of
your mind. He's no menace now.'

Once again, all of the anger, the frustration, the galling
bitterness, came flooding over Brad as he listened to the
other's faintly mocking tones. As before, it prompted him
into action before he had intended to move. Jerking the
second Colt from its holster, he pushed himself to his feet,
moved out into the open, covering the three men standing in front of the hut, the faint glow of firelight spilling
out through the open door, limming their figures.

'That's where you're wrong,' he said thinly, his voice
carrying well in the silence. 'Seems you shouldn't have
trusted Frye to do your dirty work for you. I had him
figured for the man who betrayed me all those years ago.
Seems I was wrong and I've got you to thank for it. Now
just step forward a little so I know the identity of the
yellow-livered coyote before I shoot you down.'

The three men stood there in stunned, shocked
silence, staring across at him, their faces dim grey blurs in
the starlight. Then the man called Clarke said tightly: 'You
got no call to kill us, mister. We don't know you.'

'You're ridin' with this *hombre*, ain't you?' Brad gritted.
'Drop those rifles now, before I decide to shoot you down.
I've been through a little too much to think twice about it.'

For a long second they hesitated. Brad thought he
saw the thought of action in the stance of one of them.
Then they opened their hands and let the weapons fall
at their feet.

'That's better.' Brad made his way forward slowly. 'Seems to me from what I found that you've had a spot of trouble here. Could be that your band has been broken and scattered for good.'

There was no answer from any of them as they eyed him in sullen silence. He grinned mirthlessly. Then his weapons swung to cover the two men standing a little apart from the third. 'Like you say, I've got no score to settle with you. I'm no lawman, although it would give me the greatest pleasure to kill you. But this is the man I'm after. When I've finished with him it will all be over. You two got your horses around here someplace?'

'Sure,' grunted Clarke hoarsely. 'They're tethered at the side of the cabin.'

'Then unfasten your gunbelts, and saddle up. Ride out of here before I change my mind about letting you go.' As they turned after unbuckling their gunbelts, the third man said with a note of desperation in his tone. 'Don't listen to him, either of you! I know him. He'll shoot you both in the back as soon as you're mounted up. It's a trick.'

The men paused at that, then Clarke said tightly: 'Could be you're right. But I'm leavin'. You seem to have bought yourself some big trouble here and I want no part of it whatever.'

Brad's smile widened. This was just what he had expected. These men owed their primary allegiance to themselves. They would sell their gun to the highest bidder, but if things got too tough they would ride out to save their own skins, if the chance were offered to them, rather than stay behind and fight somebody else's battle. Especially if the odds seemed turned against them.

Brad watched as they moved towards their waiting mounts, climbed up into the saddle and edged their way slowly past the hut, pausing to look down for a moment at Calder and the other man. Then they started out along the narrow trail that cut down from the valley, into the shadowy trees in the distance.

'Come back here,' roared the other at the top of his voice. He swung around as if to run after them.

'It's no use,' Brad called sharply. 'You're finished. They won't stick around and risk their necks just for you. You've reached the end of the trail right here. Now back up and move into the hut. Move!'

He saw the other's shoulders sag as he turned to move back. Brad went forward after him, taking his glance away from the two dark figures riding down towards the far end of the valley. This was a mistake. One of the men – in the darkness it was impossible to say which – turned suddenly in his saddle, whipped out a rifle which must have been in the scabbard there, threw it to his shoulder and snapped off a rapid shot at Brad. The slug missed, hummed past his head into the distance.

Jerking himself around, Brad caught a swift glimpse of the other man running for the cabin. Swiftly, he sent a shot into the half-open door to warn the other, heard the wood splinter as the slug tore into it, saw too late that the other had not intended to run into the shelter of the hut. Instead, he swerved away, running to where the third horse was tethered, just visible in the deep shadows.

Brad sent two more shots at the other, but the man was in the saddle and at the same moment the horse reared up on its hind legs and the bullets went wild. Before he could fire again the horse had taken a quick lunge forward, which took it almost to a dead run in the next few yards. Brad hurried the next shot, knew that he had missed even as he fired. The following moment, horse and rider had plunged into the brush, gone from sight, although he could still hear the crash of their headlong flight through the pines.

Cursing himself for his folly, he ran swiftly to where he had left his own mount, knowing that the other would not stop until he was miles away from this place and he might never find him again. How could he have missed at that range? he thought angrily. He had the other there in front of him, could have pulled the trigger and dropped him without any fuss and he would have solved everything. Yet something had held him back. What could that have been? The inner decency which would not allow him to gun down an unarmed man? The desire to make the other crawl and cringe even more before he died? It was something he was not sure about and he put the thoughts out of his mind as he cut down the narrow wrinkle in the ground, falling and stumbling in his haste, cutting and scratching his hands on the longthorn which grew in profusion here, but not feeling it.

At length he came to the clump of tall bushes where his horse was standing patiently. Swiftly, he swung up into the saddle, kicked hard at the animal's flanks, raking spurs cruelly across them, oblivious to everything now but the savage desire to catch up with that man, to hunt him down, through the trees and hills, out across the desert if needs be.

He raced past the shadowy shapes of the deserted hut with the flicker of firelight just visible through the open doorway, cut down into the trees, following the trail of broken branches and crushed undergrowth. Even in the darkness it was easy to follow. The trail led him downgrade for perhaps half a mile, then angled out until it came upon the main trail running through the hills. A quick glance told him that the man was heading east in the direction of the desert.

Half-an-hour later, as he came out of the tall pines, he saw the cloud of dust in the distance where the other was spurring away from him. The other had an advantage now. His mount was fresh, whereas Brad's was tired after the long day's pull across the desert. But inspite of this, as the minutes went by, he saw that he was gradually closing the

distance. He splashed across a low stream that bordered
the rough ground and up to where the alkaline dust lifted
and fell in a series of rolling swells, like a great ocean all
about him. Gigantic rock formations lifted from it, gleaming eerily in the starshine. His quarry had moved around
one of them about a mile ahead. As he rode, Brad kept his
eye on the tall butte, watching for the other to ride out
from behind it. When he saw no further dust he was
puzzled for a moment. It seemed scarcely credible that the
other would stop, would turn and fight even if he had a
weapon with him, when he had quite an appreciable lead.

As he approached the tall butte he circled more widely
around it than the other had done, eyes wary, determined
not to make any more mistakes. He could make out no
sign of the other and yet it was certain that he had not
ridden on. He must have stopped there, dismounted and
climbed up the tall rocky face of red sandstone, was probably cowering behind the boulders, drawing a bead on
him with a high-powered rifle.

Cautiously he rode closer, taut and straight in the
saddle, feeling the flesh on his body creep and the small
hairs on the back of his neck prickle uncomfortably.

Three hundred yards from the nearer edge of the butte
and a rifle barked loudly, the shattering echo splintering
the silence into a thousand pieces. The slug hit the
ground a couple of yards from his mount, kicking up a
spurt of dust. He reined up quickly. The distance was too
far for a Colt to be used with any degree of accuracy,
whereas the other could easily pick him off with that rifle.

Dropping from the saddle, he darted forward, throwing
caution to the winds. The rifle barked once more. This
time he felt the scorching heat of the bullet as it whirred
past his cheek. Dropping flat, he wriggled forward,
presenting a more difficult target in the darkness now, his
body blending with the dust. The Colt in his right hand,
he began to crawl slowly forward, watching the rocks

ahead of him, pale grey in the dimness.

Fifty yards to go. *All right,* he thought tightly, *let's feel him out. Let's see if he's any good when it comes to fighting in the open, when there are only two of us, man against man, gun against gun, with only one going to get up and walk away from the encounter.*

He edged behind a low ridge, felt for a rock, closed his fingers around one and tossed it, back-handed, to his right. The rifle sounded once more. This time he was able to see the orange-bright muzzle flash, knew that the other had worked his way up on to the lower ledge, some thirty feet above the smooth floor of the desert. From there he commanded an excellent view of the ground below him, but it also meant that he would have to expose himself somewhat to fire downwards. Brad smiled to himself in the darkness. In spite of the fact that the other was up there, under cover, he felt some of the tension go out of his body, felt his limbs and his mind loosen a little. Now he knew for sure where the other was, he could make his plans accordingly. He inched forward a dozen yards, then stopped, threw another stone, a little further this time, grinned as he heard the bark of the rifle and moved off to his right, creeping forward silently, catlike in the shadows.

'I know you're down there, Calder. But you won't get me. You can't move up any closer without me seeing you and this rifle will stop you before you can get in range of your Colts '

Keep talking, Brad thought savagely, *all you're doing is guiding me to you, making things a heap easier for me.*

He reached the bottom of the sheer face of the butte. A dozen yards away he could just make out the other's horse, standing slack-hipped. It led him to the narrow trail which the other had taken when he had clambered up on to that rocky ledge. Cautiously, making no sound, he began the climb. Occasionally the other yelled something, clearly hoping to make him give himself away. There was a note of growing desperation in the man's voice now. He was becoming more and more afraid. The waiting was telling on him more than on Brad. Sooner or later he would break and give himself away, do something rash. Pulling himself over the sharp-edged lips of the ledge, he could hear the man now, not more than a score of feet away. A boot scraped on loose rock. A stone went bouncing down the sheer sandstone face to the desert below. The other must have realized that he was very close to the edge and was moving back, scrabbling on his hands and knees.

He could picture the man beginning to panic inside, knowing that he was somewhere close by, knowing that he had made a mistake in stopping here where the way out was blocked. Brad pressed close, keeping his head and shoulders well down. As yet he could not see the other, although he could hear his harsh breathing and the rattle of the gun against the rocks.

Then he saw him, a dark humped shadow, crouched down behind one of the tall, upthrusting boulders, his back to Brad, eyes staring out over the smooth face of the desert below him, evidently straining to see him; knowing that the longer it took for him to spot his pursuer, the more dangerous the situation was for him. He had been shooting at shadows and he could not have much more ammunition left.

Easing himself up, resting one hand on the rock beside him, Brad levelled the Colt on the spot between the other's shoulders and said sharply: 'All right, drop that rifle and turn round slowly.'

He saw the other stiffen, saw his shoulder muscles lump under his jacket. For a long second it looked as if the other had not heard him or if he had, he did not intend to obey.

'Drop it, I say!' Brad snapped. 'Or I'll shoot you in the back.'

'You wouldn't do that,' said the other in a low, strained

voice. 'You've got too much honour. You see I know you, Cap'n Calder. I know how you work. You have not spent your life since the war as I have. I've learned all of the tricks. It wouldn't worry me in the least to shoot a man down who hadn't got a gun. But you would have to —'

The words were a feint to cover up what the other meant to do. He bit off the sentence, swung round, bringing up the barrel of the Winchester, as he fell back. The slug scorched along Brads' arm, just touching the flesh, hit the rocks behind him and screeched off into the night with the scream of tortured metal. The Colt in his hand went off thunderously as he squeezed the trigger. He felt the weapon buck against his wrist. The rifle went flying from the other's hand as the bullet smashed his wrist. He uttered a loud, harsh yelp of agony, caught at his hand, the blood dripping between his fingers.

Swiftly Brad stepped forward, caught the other by the hair and tilted his head back, ignoring the man's sharp intake of breath as the pain lanced through his arm. Now it was his turn to feel the sharp numbing shock as he stared down into the other's face. The years had scarcely touched it and recognition was immediate, yet several seconds fled before he realized that he wasn't dreaming.

'You!' he said tautly, and the single word was like an oath.

'Now you know.' Denson stared up at him, his lips drawn back so that his teeth showed in a snarl. 'You thought I'd been killed when the Yankees attacked the train, didn't you? It was so easy to fool you. That first night out on the trail after you'd told me the route we were to take, it was so simple to pass the information on to one of the men who was waiting close by, ready to ride hell for leather, to our forces waiting to the north.'

Brad stared down at him in tight-lipped silence for a long moment. The mocking smile on the other's face burned into him. 'You!' he said thinly. 'You did it! Riding along with us, knowing that you were going to come out of it alive, that you'd just play dead while all of the others would be killed.' He thrust down savagely at the other, pushing his face into the ground. 'You're not fit to die by a bullet. Hanging's the only way for you.'

He released his hold, stepped back, filled with a sudden fury. All of the hate came boiling up to the surface now, urging him to kill the other now, to get it all over and done with. He wanted to kick the other savagely on the face, to beat his body into a senseless pulp, to make him suffer even more than he was at the moment with the agony of his smashed wrist. Then the anger went out of him. He knew that he would take the other back and the law would take its course with him. Even though vengeance was his, he would not take it.

'All right,' he said tautly. 'On your feet. We're going back into town. I reckon there'll be some kind of justice waiting for you there, even if it is at the end of a rope. You don't even deserve that kind of finish.'

Slowly, the other made to push himself to his feet. Brad moved forward and bent to pick up the fallen Winchester from where it had dropped. In that moment, Denson moved. His unharmed hand reached down towards his belt. There was the faint glitter of starlight on the blade of the knife. Then his hand was moving behind his head, ready to throw. Swiftly, instinctively, Brad lifted the rifle in one hand, pointed the weapon at the other, his finger on the trigger and squeezed it gently. The gun bucked in his hand as the recoil lashed along his arm. For a moment, Denson teetered there on his toes, as if trying to reach up to the stars. There was a look of numbed surprise on his face, a look which slowly washed away into an expression of great wonder as his legs gave under him and he fell back, his head striking the rocks behind him. Limply, his body flopped over on to its side, his face upturned, the eyes staring unseeing at the bright stars.

Brad touched him with his boot, felt the looseness in him, knew that he was dead, that the men who had ridden with him along the trail of death so long ago could finally sleep quiet and easy in their graves wherever they might be, that they had now been avenged.

Slowly, picking his way carefully, he climbed down the steep slope, caught up the reins of Denson's horse, led it to where his own stood out in the desert, then climbed up stiffly into the saddle, feeling the deep emptiness in him. There was none of the elation he had expected to feel once he had met this man and killed him. His brain felt strangely hollow, all of the energy gone, all of the hate which had dominated and controlled him, burnt away. Maybe, sometime, there would be something else to replace it, something else for which to live, to make each new day an adventure. He thought of Janet Frye, of what she had said, of how she had looked to him and in spite of the numb coldness in his mind, something stirred and fanned a flame deep within him.

Around him, there was nothing but the deep and remote stillness that seemed to stretch away to the very limits of the world. He could feel it closing in on him, dark and tangible and oddly soothing. He rode slowly towards the east where, in a few hours, the first flush of dawn would show, grey and red, where the sun would come up on a day which would be different from those he had known for almost as long as he could remember. A day when the hate would have been washed from his mind; a day when he could, for the first time in so long, ride with his head held high and look his fellow men in the face.

When the dawn did finally break, it found him riding through the tall pines a couple of miles to the north of the Lazy J ranch. He had already cut through the boundary fence, was now on the spread itself. The aromatic smell of the pines was sharp in his nostrils as the little wind of the night blew itself out. The deep stillness intensified. By the

time he was urging his tired mount into the dusty courtyard, men were coming from the bunkhouse, eyeing him
curiously as he reined up in front of the door of the ranch
house.

Stiffly, he got down trom the saddle, slapped the horse
on the flanks, sent it through the gate of the corral and
then tied the gate up again, half turning towards the
house.

He saw her standing on the steps of the porch, face
turned towards him. She said softly: 'You through now,
Brad?

He nodded. 'It's finished now. I thought I'd come back
for that job you promised me.' The way he said it struck
her powerfully and she did not move away at the pressure
of his hands as he stepped up beside her on the porch.